TANTALIZE

Marie Tuhart

https://www.marietuhart.com/

TANTALIZE

Wicked Sanctuary: Surrender your inhibitions.

When her college lover introduced her to the intense and sensual pleasure of the world he'd grown to love, Dani Wright panicked and ran. Now, older and wiser, she's returned home to take the reins of her grandfather's landscaping business and enjoys the occasional dip into the life Wicked Sanctuary offers. Until her college lover shows up.

Gabriel Quinn has never forgotten Dani or the way things ended between them. He blames himself. When he sees her at Wicked Sanctuary, he's got a chance to make things right—if she'll let him. He loves her independent spirit and must tread carefully to keep from inhibiting her playful nature.

Can these two make a relationship work, especially when Dani is harboring a secret that could destroy their newfound love?

ACKNOWLEGMENTS

There are several people I want to thank for supporting me through this book:

Laurie, thank you for keeping me sane while writing this book.

Red Quill Editing team, you are the best team to work with. Your snark at Gabriel made me laugh.

Publisher's Note: This book contains a dominant male, spunky heroine, very stubborn characters, and sexy situations.

To My Readers:

This book contains elements of the BDSM lifestyle that are only true to life in this book. There are various relationship dynamics in the lifestyle, which are decided between the people involved. While I have researched and talked with people in the lifestyle, this is my take on how my characters choose to live.

If you decide to explore the lifestyle yourself, please remember to always be safe. Never go home with someone you don't know. Attend a munch or a small get-together first to see if this is something you want in your life. Reading and living are very different.

There is no mention of the coronavirus that exists in our world right now. I purposely left it out. This is a place for you to escape.

Enjoy.

Chapter 1

Dani Wright secured her long black hair into a ponytail and slipped on the pink and white wristband. She glanced at herself in the mirror and admired the way she looked in the corset and boy shorts. After making sure all her belongings were in the locker, she shut the door and secured it, walked out of the bathroom and to reception. After she finished her shift at the reception desk, she'd head into Wicked Sanctuary proper and maybe play tonight.

"Evening, Ralph." She smiled at him. Ralph was great to work with.

Ralph turned and grinned at her. "Hey Dani. Looks like we'll have a full house tonight with the Fourth of July party."

Dani sat on the padded chair behind the desk. "I figured as much. Wicked Sanctuary parties are always well attended."

"That they are."

She logged into the computer and prepared her station as people would start arriving in about ten minutes.

"I'd like to try something different tonight," Ralph said. "I'll do the computer checks, then people can sign in with you and go on their way. This way the line will move faster."

"Whatever works for you." Ralph had been doing this a lot longer than she had and doing it alone, so she deferred to him. "Sounds like a plan."

It was going to be hectic for about the first thirty minutes, then things would calm down. Calm down. Dani took a deep breath. Maybe now her life would calm down a little bit.

She'd lived with her grandparents for two months since her grandfather's heart attack, but her grandmother kept pushing her to get out on her own, insisting she was too young to be stuck in the house with them. She needed to get out of the tiny apartment she'd settled on and into a more secure building, and finally, there was a vacancy in the apartment building she wanted to live in.

Dani signed the lease for the new place before she got to the club tonight, and the apartment manager had told her she could move in right away. Now, she had to pack, get everything out of the old place, and clean it.

Ralph unlocked the door to find people already waiting. Oh yes, they were going to be busy tonight. Good. That would keep her mind off moving and everything she needed to do this weekend and over the next week.

* * * *

Gabriel Quinn stepped out of his SUV and shut the door. The parking lot was packed tonight. It was a good thing Max was expanding it along with the club. In a way, Gabriel wasn't surprised at the turnout, as this was a members only party.

He sauntered toward the front door, startled to see a small line, but it seemed to be moving quickly. Gabriel didn't care how fast the line moved. He hadn't been interested in playing lately, and he knew why.

Dani.

She'd been home a year. An entire year, and he'd only seen her at Kleinman's book store's grand opening and at Sweet & Savory. His stomach had been tied in knots ever since. How had she managed to steer clear of him all that time?

He assumed once her grandfather recovered, she'd go back to San Francisco. He was wrong. And it was unexpected how her staying had affected him. Did she even think of him?

Gabriel shook his head. He hadn't been to Wicked Sanctuary in months. His heart wasn't in it. Though he'd tried to play with a couple of the club subs, he wanted to play with Dani. College had ended that. He'd introduced her to kink only to have her freak out.

He wondered why she hadn't returned to her old life by now. It would be better if she did. Still, he hadn't been able to let go of the frustration. Drawn to Dani like no one else, he'd never be able to play with her, in the club or otherwise. She didn't like his lifestyle.

Tonight, he needed to stop thinking about her and start thinking about himself again. Get back in the game, and that was exactly why he'd come to this party.

As the line moved, Gabriel stepped in front of Ralph's station.

"Good evening," Ralph said. "I've got you checked in. Just sign in at the next station, and you're set."

"Thanks." Gabriel stepped in front of the next computer and waited for the woman to glance up. When she did, he froze. "Dani?" What the hell was she doing here? Her eyes grew wide, and she leaned back. A second later, her expression was blank.

"Hello, Sir. If you'd please sign in, you can go through."

Her voice was calm and steady, and it irked Gabriel she could be that way. What the fuck was she wearing? The deep blue corset enhanced her breasts and showed off her creamy skin. His body was already going from cold to hot and back again. He signed his name on the pad and glared at her. "What are you doing here?"

"Working, Sir."

Sir? A BDSM club was the last place on earth he expected to see Dani. Gabriel opened his mouth when Ralph interrupted.

"Is there a problem?"

"Nope, I have him all signed in," Dani said, glancing at the computer screen.

Gabriel didn't move. Couldn't move. Dani didn't belong here. Kink scared the crap out of her, and he was having a hard time wrapping his head around the fact that she was here. Except—that outfit and her band. More confused than ever, Gabriel stared at Dani. He should haul her out of her chair, march her to her car, and send her home.

A masculine hand gripped his arm. "Come with me, Gabriel." Max guided Gabriel away from the registration desk.

Gabriel didn't protest. He was still trying to process finding Dani in a BDSM club. Something wasn't right. Max led Gabriel into his office and pushed the door almost all the way closed.

Max stared at him. "Why are you so surprised to see Dani here?"

Gabriel stared right back at Max as it hit him. Dani had to be a member to sit at that registration desk. He couldn't see Max hiring someone who wasn't familiar with kink or had issues with kink. "How long has she been a member?"

"She joined right after she came home." Max continued to watch him with those knowing eyes of his. "She took the classes and asked where she could help out. Is this going to be an issue?"

"Damn right it's going to be an issue." Gabriel paced around the confines of Max's office. "Dani does not belong here. Kink is not her thing."

"And you know this how?" Max continued to stare at him.

"It doesn't matter." He wasn't going to explain what happened. That was between him and Dani. "She doesn't belong here."

"Dani mentioned to me the two of you had a past together in college, but I can assure you, she doesn't have any issues with kink. Her club trainer would have told me."

Gabriel went from cold to blazing hot in a second. "Who trained her?" While everyone who went through the classes had a trainer, he wanted to beat the crap out of Dani's.

"Bennett. He never indicated any issue. Dani had recommendations from San Francisco."

Gabriel drew his hand through his hair. "None of this makes sense." Had he entered an alternate reality? That was the only explanation, because there was no way his Dani would be here. Maybe he should have come to the club sooner instead of taking a break.

"It makes perfect sense to me. So, you have a choice to make." Max crossed his arms over his chest. "You can go into the club and enjoy the party, or you can go home."

Shock flowed through Gabriel at Max's ultimatum. But he shouldn't have been surprised. Max was very protective of the women in the club. Hell, Max was protective no matter what. "I'm staying." If Dani walked into the club, he'd corner her and find out what the hell she was doing there. Then he'd escort her to her vehicle. If she left before he could catch her, he'd find her, and they'd have the same talk.

"Very well." Max pulled open his office door.

Gabriel glanced down the hall and saw Dani talking and smiling as Bennett checked in. His hackles went up. Why would Dani play here when she wouldn't play with him in college? It didn't make sense. Gabriel forced his irritation away and went to change. There would be plenty of time to talk with her when she finished her job. Provided she didn't run. Because he wasn't done with her, not by a long shot.

* * * *

Dani smiled as the couple walked away, but her stomach churned. It hadn't stopped since Gabriel walked in. The look on his face when he saw her. She'd fought to keep her features neutral, and it hadn't been easy.

She knew they'd eventually meet up, but she hadn't expected his astonished expression or the shocked look in his eyes. She didn't think she could still startle Gabriel. He'd moved on, found someone else. At least, that's what her brain had told her all these years. The ghost of a smile touched her lips at the revelation she could still affect him. It was nice to know she had that in her arsenal.

"Go ahead on into the club," Ralph said. "Mostly everyone is here, and the few stragglers that come in I can handle by myself."

"Thanks, Ralph." Dani shut down her computer and stood up. She smoothed her hair back with a shaky hand. Maybe she should freshen up. No. She straightened. Gabriel being here meant nothing.

Their relationship ended a long time ago, and she wasn't rehashing that. She reached for the door handle, telling herself over and over again they were done, willing her body to stop shaking, to stop reacting to Gabriel. The past was the past. At least she was trying to convince herself of that.

She walked into the main area and made a beeline for the sub area. She was glad to see not only other subs sitting there, but her best friend, Allyson. Zeke was on duty tonight. She sat down on the sofa next to Allyson.

"Finally. I thought you might be stuck at the desk for most of the night," Allyson said.

"Only until things calmed down and Ralph could handle it by himself." Dani leaned closer to her friend. "Did you know Gabriel would be here tonight?"

Allyson shifted in her seat. "I knew it was a possibility. He's come in a few times, but usually after you leave."

"That answers why I haven't seen him here before." While Dani played only one night a week, the other night she worked the desk with Ralph for a few hours. She was surprised she and Gabriel hadn't run into each other at the club before now. While the club wasn't huge, it was big enough that you didn't always see everyone, and she'd only been working the desk with Ralph for a few weeks.

"What did he say when he saw you? Allyson asked.

"He asked what I was doing here." When Ralph trained her on the computers, she'd seen his name. It was a good thing the encounter happened tonight; they were so busy, Gabriel couldn't make a scene.

There was so much emotion on his face and in his voice. They really hadn't talked, not at Kleinman's or at Sweet & Savory when she told him to walk away. Would he have made a scene here? She thought he might, even if it was against the rules, but Master Max led him away before he could. She'd changed since he sprang kink on her in college.

She longed for something she could never have with

Gabriel. A life. She didn't doubt for a minute that Gabriel was still as anti-relationship as he was in college. No, that wasn't quite true. He was anti-commitment when they graduated four years ago.

"You really haven't given him the time of day since you came back. Even at the bookstore opening, you avoided him like the plague. And I believe you only talked to him for a minute that day at Sweet & Savory."

"I know. And I have yet to explain why." Dani rubbed her tummy and looked at her friend. It was time. "I told you about the love affair I had when I was in college."

"Yes. I know you were a little heartbroken when he left you, but you didn't want to talk about it, and I respected your wishes. But..." Allyson's eyes lit up. "You said at Kleinman's your old boyfriend was there; I assumed he was one of the construction guys. It was Gabriel."

The astonishment in Allyson's voice almost caused Dani to smile. "The very one. I won't go into details right now, but let's just say we parted on some very bad terms, and when I graduated, he was one of the reasons I took the job in San Francisco."

Allyson whistled. "We have to have a girl's night."

"Agreed." She owed it to her friend to tell her everything. "I do have some good news. I signed the lease on my new apartment today."

"That's wonderful. I know you've been wanting into that new complex."

"I'll be honest; I got lucky."

"Fantastic. Just let me know, and Zeke and I will gather up some muscle to get you all moved in."

Dani grinned. "I'll take the help to pack things up, but I'm still going to need some things."

"So Sunday, we get to go shopping?"

Dani laughed. "Yes, unless you can spare some time tomorrow?" She knew Allyson kept the weekends open for Zeke.

"I'll talk with Zeke. I'm sure he can spare me for one Saturday. But it will probably have to be the afternoon. We'll be here late tonight."

"Not a problem." Dani fought to keep the envy out of her voice. She was glad her friend had found a man to count on and one who did not bow down to her snobby family.

"Excuse me," a male voice said.

Dani looked up to see Austin, one of the club Doms, standing to her right. His short blond hair was styled in spikes, and his aquamarine eyes flashed as he smiled.

"Dani, would you like to do some bondage with me tonight?"

"Yes, Sir, I would."

Allyson started coughing, and Dani looked at her.

"If you could give me a minute, please, Sir."

"Of course. I'll be waiting nearby." Austin moved away, and Dani turned to Allyson.

"What's going on?" Dani asked.

"Are you sure it's a good idea to play with Gabriel here?"

"It's fine. Trust me when I say Gabriel doesn't want to play with me." Dani believed that even though she was the one who rejected kink all those years ago. But she was a different woman now, and it was obvious from what Gabriel said that he felt she didn't belong in the club. She'd changed, but apparently, he hadn't.

"Are you sure about that?" Allyson stared at her.

"Yes." Dani stood up and smoothed her hands down her blue corset and black boy shorts. "I'll see you later." She walked over to Austin and placed her hand in his.

She'd played with him before, and he knew bondage. They were very good match.

A tremor of apprehension slipped through her body. What would Gabriel think when he saw her play? Would he want to be the one tying her up?

No. Gabriel didn't do commitment and probably had a sub. He wouldn't care about her. They were long done. If only she could convince her heart of that.

* * * *

Gabriel looked around the club for Dani. He hadn't seen her so far, but the club was full tonight. He checked the sub area earlier; it'd been empty.

He thought about going back out to the lobby, but Max's words came back to him. Gabriel had wanted to explain to Max how he knew Dani didn't belong there. He needed to have the conversation with Dani first. He wandered around, keeping an eye out for her long black hair and the blue corset she was wearing.

Damn, she looked good in that corset. The way the material cupped her breasts and pushed them up. His body heated. A group of people were gathering around one of the bondage stations, and he decided to head in that direction. Why not? It might take his mind off other things.

Austin was on stage. When he was ready, he turned and held his hand out to a sub. Oh, hell no. Gabriel didn't stop to think. He couldn't stop himself. He marched toward the stage. "Austin, I need to talk with you for a moment."

The blond-haired Dom tilted his head and nodded, but it was Dani who spoke. "There is no need, Sir."

Austin hesitated and leaned down, whispered into Dani's ear, saying something that made her giggle. Gabriel's hackles rose. He was the only one that was supposed to make Dani laugh. Except she'd rejected him.

And now, suddenly, she was into kink? No. Gabriel refused to believe that. What game was she playing? Her fear of kink had been real and devastating to their relationship.

"What's up, Gabriel?" Austin asked, walking to the edge of the stage.

Gabriel took Austin in from head to toe. He was dressed like most of them. Dark pants, open shirt, and loafers. "Sorry to interrupt and butt in, but you shouldn't be playing with Dani."

Austin's eyebrows rose. "Why is that? We've played together before, and there's been no issue."

Gabriel's temper rose. Austin had played with Dani before? How many other men had she played with? Dammit. She'd played with other Doms, but rejected him in the café. The little green monster of jealousy grew in him.

"You may have played with her before, but I wasn't in the club when you did so."

Austin frowned. "Did I miss something? She's wearing a pink and white wristband so she isn't taken."

Gabriel wanted to say, yes, she was taken, but he didn't have the right. That was one of the tenets of the lifestyle, and he wouldn't betray that. "No, she's not taken that I know of, but Dani doesn't belong in the kink world."

Austin rubbed his forehead. "I don't know where you've been, but obviously you've not seen Dani play before. We're quite good together, and I'm sorry if you have an issue with it. But that's not my problem or Dani's."

Gabriel opened his mouth when a strong hand gripped his shoulder. "Gabriel's just being cautious. He doesn't realize that Dani is a big girl and can take care of herself," Max said. "Go do your scene before the crowd gets too restless."

"Thank you, Max." Austin walked over to Dani.

"Before you say a single word, this is what I warned you about. I don't know why you can't respect her choices."

Another Dom/sub tenet that Gabriel had lived by up until now. He hated to admit it, but Max was right. Still, worry sat in the pit of his stomach like lead. "Can I at least talk to her before they start the scene?" Maybe he could talk her out of it.

"Gabriel, under normal circumstances, I'd tell you no way and might even ask you to leave. Just this once, and *only* this one time, and in view of our friendship, I will ask her, but it's up to her, and you are going to live with whatever choice *she* makes. Are we clear?"

"Crystal clear."

Max walked onto the stage and motioned to Dani. She walked over to him and was about to kneel when Max said something.

Gabriel's stomach clenched. What was wrong with him? He'd seen many subs kneel in front of Max, so why did this bother him so much? Because it was Dani. Dani who had run from him when he tried any sort of kink with her in college. Dani who thought he was crazy and out of his mind. Dani who was now in Wicked Sanctuary. Why was she here? And, if now, why not then? With him?

Max called Austin over to where he and Dani stood. The trio talked. Austin leaned down and kissed Dani on the cheek before walking away. Max helped Dani from the stage, and together, they walked over to him.

Dani's brown eyes flashed daggers at him as she came closer. "Dani has agreed to talk with you," Max said.

"Alone," Gabriel insisted.

Max looked at Dani. "It's fine, Master Max. We'll be over by the quiet area. If I need help, I'll call out my safe word."

"All right," Max said.

Dani turned and made her way to the quiet area. Luckily, it was empty right now. Gabriel followed, and when he arrived, she put her hands on her hips.

"What the hell is your problem?" she asked.

"You freaked out in college when I tried to introduce you to kink." *Freaked* was an apt descriptor; she'd started shaking and stared at him like he'd gone crazy.

"Things have changed. You need to get that through your head." She rubbed her fingers over her forehead.

"You were gone for over three years. Things don't change that fast." It could have been thirty years as far as he was concerned. Dani was Dani. She couldn't have changed that much.

Dani blew out a breath. "Gabriel, if I had asked you to play with me tonight, would you have?"

He didn't even hesitate. "No." She didn't belong in the lifestyle. She was afraid of it.

"And there you have it. We're not compatible. Never have been. We have nothing to say to each other."

"I think we have a lot to say to each other." What was going on with her? This wasn't the Dani he knew. Yes, she had always been spunky; she'd speak her mind, but the only time they'd really had an argument was when it came to kink.

"No, we don't." She started to walk around him, and without thinking, Gabriel grasped her arm. "Red!"

Gabriel dropped his hand in shock. She'd used her safe word? Max and Damon were at her side in an instant.

"That's it," Max said. "This conversation is over. Gabriel, if you can't deal with Dani being here, then you need to leave."

Gabriel ran a hand over his face. "I'm sorry, Dani," Gabriel said. "I don't know what came over me." He knew better than to grab a sub. Any sub in the club. Dani was right to call her safe word. But that didn't make him feel any better.

"It doesn't matter." Dani glanced up at Max. "May I go back to Austin now?"

Max nodded.

"May I escort you?" Damon asked holding out his hand.

"Thank you, Master Damon."

Gabriel watched Damon escort Dani back to where Austin waited, his stomach still churning and anger at himself bouncing around in his head.

"Are we going to have any more problems?" Max asked.

"No, Max. We won't." Gabriel walked away from Max and to the bar. Since this was a members only party, Max was allowing alcohol, but only if you weren't going to play. "Whiskey. Neat," Gabriel told Noah.

"Certainly. I have to give you another wristband."

"Not a problem." Gabriel held out his arm, and Noah slipped a magenta band around his wrist. It was like one of those hospital bands you weren't going to get off without a pair of scissors.

A minute later, his whiskey was placed in front of him. Gabriel picked it up and knocked it back. He set the empty glass down before he turned and walked out of the club. There was no way he could stay and watch Dani play. But they were going to talk. He would make sure of it.

* * * *

"Thank you for escorting me back, Master Damon," Dani said as they reached the stage.

"You're welcome." Damon left her with a grin, and Dani turned to the stage.

Austin was there, squatting at the edge of the stage. "Are you okay?"

"I'm not." While she wanted to play, her gut clenched, and her hands were shaking. "I'm sorry. I don't think I can do this right now, Sir."

"There's nothing to be sorry about. None of this was your doing." Austin looked over her shoulder. "Your friends are looking very concerned. Why don't you let them know you're okay. We can play another night."

"Thank you, Sir." Dani turned and made her way back to the quiet area. Austin was right. They could play another night. She was too rattled from Gabriel's anger to enjoy anything at the moment. Why had he reacted like that?

Sierra, Crystal, Tessa, and Allyson were sitting on the edge of their seats, their gazes glued to Dani's face.

Allyson stood up and guided Dani over to a sofa, keeping her arm around her even as they sat down together.

"I've never heard you safeword before," Sierra said.

Dani closed her eyes and took a deep breath. "It was an extreme measure." She was still surprised she'd done that to Gabriel. Not because he grabbed her arm, but because he wouldn't listen. His touch did funny things to her. Exciting things she didn't want to think about. Her nerves came alive at his touch. But Gabriel was the one who'd rejected her, and she needed to remind him of that.

"Do I need to talk to Max about not allowing Gabriel into the club anymore?" Sierra asked.

"Absolutely not." Dani sat up from her position on the sofa. "Gabriel has as much right to be here as I do. Either he deals with me being here or he doesn't. But I won't have him banned." She meant what she said.

"And what if he can't deal?" Crystal asked.

Dani shook her head. "Not my problem." And it wasn't.

"You should've seen Damon's face when you yelled your safeword," Tessa said. "He couldn't get to you fast enough."

"I've caused a mess tonight." Dani shook her head and slumped against the sofa. What was she going to do?

Allyson put her arm around Dani and squeezed her shoulders.

"There is a history between you and Gabriel, isn't there?" Sierra asked.

"If that wasn't obvious by what happened, I don't know what could be." Dani had a decision to make. How much did she say tonight? Why was she even hesitating? It was time to get the story out. "Gabriel and I were lovers in college."

Allyson tightened her hold on Dani's shoulders. Dani was appreciative of her friend's support. "We broke up shortly after Gabriel tried to introduce me to kink. At the time, it wasn't something I was interested in."

"Well, that's not unusual," Crystal observed.

"I think my reaction might've been a little over the top." Dani would take responsibility for her own actions, but she wouldn't take responsibility for Gabriel's.

"I've never seen Gabriel act like that," Tessa said.

The other women agreed, and Dani wasn't surprised. While Gabriel was very protective, she hadn't expected him to react the way he had. Was that why she avoided him all this time? She'd only come home because of her grandfather's heart attack, then stayed because he could no longer run the landscape business. And she wasn't about to let the family business die because she was afraid of an old lover.

"Gabriel is intense, but he works hard and focuses on each aspect of his job," Allyson said. "I mean, he works with Zeke."

"I doubt Zeke even knows," Dani said. Why would Gabriel even mention her? They'd broken up a long time ago. It was over. Dani rubbed a hand over her heart, trying to make it understand.

"Well, since we have some time, shall we discuss what topic we're going to have at our next sub meeting?" Sarah asked.

Dani flashed Sierra a grateful smile for changing the subject and listened with half an ear as the women talked. She had some thinking to do. All of it to do with Gabriel.

* * * *

Gabriel sat in his SUV and stared out the windshield. Max was right. Dani was a member of the club, which meant she'd been through all the classes and passed the background check. She had every right to be there. Plus, she had to know what she was getting into from the classes.

He needed to wrap his head around it. Easier said than done. He started at the knock on the window and turned to the sound. Zeke stood there. Gabriel motioned him to step back, opened the door and climbed out of the vehicle.

"Are you coming back in? Or are you going to sit here all night?" Zeke asked.

"Only you could get away with saying that." Gabriel was grateful for his friend.

"That's why we're best friends. One of the Doms asked if you would give him some instructions on impact play."

"It would have to be verbal only." He held up his wrist, showing Zeke the magenta band. "While I've only had one drink and I'm in no way impaired, I won't take chances, and I won't break the rules."

"I'm sure verbal will be enough."

"Is Max okay with me coming back in?" He'd made a mess of things.

"As long as you leave Dani alone. But you do need to understand: Dani is a part of the community now."

"Yeah." Gabriel pressed the key fob to lock his truck and walked with Zeke back into the club. His apprehension at the thought of seeing Dani play increased as they entered. But Zeke directed him to the other side of the room.

"Thank you for agreeing to the instruction," the Dom said when they approached.

"Not a problem. I have to warn you, I cannot show you anything because I had a drink tonight, but I can certainly verbally walk you through whatever you want to do."

"We're just starting to play with paddles, so I want to make sure I'm not hitting her too hard or too soft."

"Okay." That was easy enough. Gabriel looked over the area. A small spanking bench was set up, and the sub stood next to it. "I would suggest starting with her clothes on and let her tell you how it feels. What kind of paddle do you have?"

The Dom invited Gabriel onto the stage and showed him everything he'd laid out. "Good selection. Let's start with the fur covered one and go from there."

"Very well." The Dom walked over to the sub and spoke with her. Within minutes, she was bent over the spanking bench. Gabriel moved closer to give instructions as needed but not so close as to interrupt the connection between Dom and sub.

For the next thirty minutes, Gabriel taught him which paddles to use and how much strength to put behind each hit. By the time they were finished, the sub was nice and relaxed, and the Dominant was happy.

Gabriel handed the Dom a blanket and gave him instructions on what type of aftercare he needed to provide. The Dom thanked him and carried his sub off stage. Gabriel turned and saw Dani.

How long had she been watching? He kept his gaze on her as she turned and walked away. Was it because she didn't want to talk to him or because of the impact play? Impact play was what had scared her back in college.

"Good instructions," Colby said.

"Thanks." Impact play could be very intense and wasn't for everyone, as he'd learned the hard way. "You make floggers for a living, and I bet you know the impact of each one." He and Colby walked over to the bar where Zeke sat.

"I do."

Gabriel signaled the bartender. "Sparkling water, if you have it."

"You got it." Within a few minutes, the bartender returned with a tall glass and set it in front of Gabriel.

He took a sip, and his muscles started to relax. He didn't want any more alcohol tonight. The one drink had been enough. Now he just had to figure out how to deal with Dani. Because he needed to deal with her being in the club and her being into kink.

* * * *

Dani wandered around the club. When she saw Gabriel re-enter, her heart sped up. She watched him and Zeke go over to a scene. When Gabriel mounted the stage, she thought he was going to give a demonstration, but instead, he only gave instructions to the Dom.

She'd moved closer to hear what he said. Her heart still fluttered at his words. Gabriel knew what he was talking about and was damned impressive. If he had taken the time years ago to explain in the detail she witnessed here, they might still be together. Her growing respect grew even more when he stopped the Dom more than once so they could discuss what was happening. And his kindness at the end of the scene, explaining to the Dom what aftercare the sub would need, reinforced to Dani that Gabriel was an excellent Dom.

Dani sighed and approached her friend.

"Allyson, I'm going to head home."

"Are you okay? It's barely midnight."

"I'm fine, just a little tired. It's been a long day."

"Okay, I'll call you in the morning about shopping after I talk with Zeke."

"Sounds good." Dani hugged her friend and made her way to the ladies' room. She opened her locker and pulled out her T-shirt. She slipped it on to conceal her corset, but her shorts were fine. It was July, after all, and warm enough not to worry about getting cold.

She gathered the rest of her things, made her way to the lobby, said good night to Ralph, and went to her car. A good thing about the club was it was away from town. She would have time to think as she drove home.

It wasn't like tonight was the first time she'd seen Gabriel since she came home. But the impact of seeing him in the club, and in full Dom mode, set a fire in her that wasn't easily quenched. She thought she'd gotten over Gabriel. Tonight showed her how wrong she was. And Gabriel?

Did it really matter? Probably not. They'd get past this incident and go on with their lives. Gabriel could never know how pivotal that night back in college had been for her.

When she entered his apartment that night, she was tired and cranky, and Gabriel told her a spanking would help her relax. Her mind flashed back to a college friend who had a boyfriend who spanked her and left bruises. So, when Gabriel said those words, she told him there was no way in hell that was going to happen.

While they fooled around in the bedroom with him tying her up and different positions, the spanking was something totally different. She wasn't proud of how she'd reacted. Dani exhaled. They probably could've worked things out if Gabriel had listened to her when she tried to explain.

That was part of the problem. Gabriel didn't always listen.

Dani pulled into her parking spot at her apartment. Life went on, and she would cope with Gabriel being in the club. The issue was: Could Gabriel?

Chapter 2

Gabriel's frustration spilled over by the end of the following week. He tried to get in contact with Dani, but she was dodging his calls. He tried to talk to Allyson and Zeke about Dani, but those two were close-mouthed, and it was driving him crazy.

It shouldn't be, but it was. He and Dani parted on bad terms. He only wanted to talk to her. Zeke had taken Gabriel aside and told him, with Dani being Allyson's best friend, there was no way Allyson would betray Dani's confidences. Gabriel understood, but he also wanted to know what was going on with Dani, to know she was all right.

Maybe a visit to her grandparents' house would help. He'd have to make it a surprise one. He'd visited them quite often when Dani was in San Francisco. Even after she came home, he visited. Interesting how he never ran into her. He'd seen little things that told him she was there: a sweater on a chair, hair ties, and a pair of shoes too small for anyone else. When the items disappeared, he'd assumed Dani had gone back to San Francisco. Her grandparents' house was definitely the place to start. Decision made, he got into his vehicle.

Gabriel pulled up outside the small house and noted the faded, dark gray paint. He'd have to mention it to Zeke. Zeke could get the paint, and Gabriel would talk with a couple of the construction guys. Between three or four of them, they could have the house primed and painted in two days.

Gabriel rapped his knuckles on the wooden door and waited. It took a couple of minutes before Maggie's smiling face came into view. "Gabriel, this is such a nice surprise." Maggie let go of the door and pulled Gabriel in for a hug.

"It's always good to see you, too, Maggie." She smelled of lavender and fresh bread, something he would always associate with her. Gabriel didn't remember his grandparents at all even though his mother insisted her parents visited him. He shook away the thoughts of his dysfunctional family.

"Come on in. Would you like some iced tea?"

"I don't want to put you to any trouble." Gabriel shut the door behind him, noting how Maggie shuffled her feet more than normal. He'd have to ask Dani about that if she'd talk to him. Maggie and Bert were getting up in age, and he worried they might need more help than they let Dani know.

"No trouble at all, dear. Bert is in the front room. Go join him, and I'll be there shortly." Maggie walked away, and Gabriel made his way to the front room. Bert looked up as he walked in.

"Gabriel."

"Hey, Bert." Gabriel waved his hands when Bert tried to stand. After Bert's heart attack a year ago, even though he'd recovered, he still tired easily, and Gabriel didn't want him straining himself. Gabriel took the chair across from Bert.

Within a few minutes, Maggie carried a tray in. Gabriel jumped up and took the tray from her, setting it on the coffee table. "Tea and some cookies," Maggie said as she put a glass in front of her husband and one in front of Gabriel.

"So, what brings you here today?" Bert asked.

"It's been a while since I saw the two of you, so I thought I'd drop by and check in. Do you need anything?" Gabriel took a sip of his tea and barely hid a grimace at the sweetness. Maggie was a little heavy-handed with the sugar.

"That's so sweet of you," Maggie said from her position next to her husband. "We're doing just fine."

"Wonderful." Gabriel glanced around the room, noting the new curtains that allowed more light into the room. "Is Dani around?"

Bert let out a gruff. "I told you Dani's mood was because of Gabriel."

"Really?" Maggie scolded him. "When did you find out she was back?"

"I knew she'd come home when Bert was in the hospital, but I thought she'd gone back to San Francisco. A little over a month ago, I saw her at the bookstore." He was on good speaking terms with both of them, so it was a puzzle to him why they stayed silent. Well, maybe not. They were protecting the little girl they'd raised since she was orphaned at age eight.

Maggie's cheeks turned pink. "Dani asked us not to tell you. I don't know what happened between you two in college. She would never talk about it. We were respecting her wishes."

Gabriel tilted his head. "I wouldn't expect you to do anything else." He was being truthful. He didn't blame them for keeping Dani's secret. They were going to keep their granddaughter safe, even from him.

"It doesn't matter anyway," Bert said. "Dani's been living on her own for several months now."

Gabriel sat back in the chair. That was news to him. He

was sure Zeke and Allyson knew, but neither had mentioned it to him. "I didn't realize that."

"We told her it was okay. I was lucky my heart attack wasn't worse than it was," Bert said. "Plus, I'm up a lot at night."

"Are you not sleeping?" That wasn't good.

Bert waved his hand. "Nothing to worry about. I got up for years at five in the morning, and it's a hard habit to break."

Gabriel released a breath. It would devastate Dani if something happened to either of her grandparents, and he'd been a fool to think she'd have glibly returned to her San Francisco life. Of course she'd stayed to take over the family landscaping business after Bert had his heart attack. Gabriel wanted to slap himself. Dani had been here all the time, and his assumptions had wasted a lot of time.

Maggie leaned over to tap Gabriel's knee, getting his attention. "We're sorry we couldn't tell you about Dani. Right now, I think she needs some privacy."

"And I get the distinct feeling you're the reason," Bert said, lasering Gabriel with a protective stare.

Gabriel took another sip of tea. "Dani and I are not back together." At least not right now, but they damn sure were going to have a talk one of these days. He stayed and talked with Maggie and Bert for another hour. He told them he noticed that the house could use a good coat of paint and not to worry. That he'd take care of it. When he stood up to go, Maggie walked into the front door and gave him another hug.

Maggie looked up at him. "You're a good man at the core, Gabriel. I don't know what Dani's reasons are for not talking to you. If I tell you where she lives, can you promise me you won't hurt her?"

"I could never hurt Dani." The response, immediate and burnt into his soul, was the truth. He never wanted to be the reason Dani was in pain. Was she now? Because of him? Clueless as to what was going on with Dani, he needed to find her now more than ever. They definitely had some things to talk about.

Maggie eyed him long and hard, finally nodding. "I guess it can't hurt to let you know where she is. She's got an apartment over on Jackson Way. That new apartment building. The fancy one."

"I know the one." He leaned down and kissed her cheek. "Thank you, Maggie." Gabriel jogged to his work truck. He knew exactly which apartment building. He'd been the architect on the project. Now, to go over there and have that talk with Dani.

* * * *

Dani blew out a breath as the small moving truck Zeke volunteered to drive pulled up with Allyson following, driving their vehicle filled with Dani's stuff. Bennett and Austin were right behind Allyson. They were the muscle, as they called themselves.

How much shopping did she and Allyson do last weekend? She didn't think it had been that much, but now she wondered. Her new apartment had two bedrooms, a family room, small dining room, and another room for storage that would eventually become her home office.

Over the next few hours, the moving truck was unloaded while she and Allyson made the beds and set up her bedroom. Once that was done, they started to work on the bathroom. They hung a new shower curtain and placed the matching sea-colored rugs on the floor.

Her phone buzzed with a text. The furniture company would be here at four. Her family room was now larger so she'd bought a better sofa, plus bookcases, side tables, and an entertainment center. There was a lot of work still to do. Thank goodness she'd shifted most of her gardening jobs to other days, and she had a good crew taking over the ones she couldn't do right away.

She glanced around the apartment. There were boxes everywhere. "Can you move these boxes into the storage room?" she asked Zeke.

"Yes, ma'am." He gave her a salute.

"I think you're livable for now," Allyson remarked as Zeke walked back into the room. "We need to be somewhere else."

"Go." She waved her hands at them. Bennett and Austin had left a half hour ago to return the rental truck. "You've both been so helpful." She hugged them. It was wonderful to have such good friends in Zeke and Allyson.

The furniture company arrived. She showed them where she wanted her new family room furniture and then went into the kitchen. She began unpacking those boxes and listened to the moving men talk and joke with each other as they carried in her purchases and set everything up. Then she heard another voice. A voice that didn't belong. She turned to see Gabriel leaning against the doorjamb to the kitchen.

"What are you doing here?" Why was she surprised? She hadn't answered his calls or texts. Her gaze took in what he was wearing. Damn, why did the man have to look so good in a t-shirt and jeans? And why did her heart speed up when she saw him?

"I like the new apartment," he said with a brazen grin.

"Ma'am, we're about done. Would you make sure we have this the way you want it," one of the delivery men said.

Dani marched to the kitchen entrance and stared at Gabriel until he stepped out of her way. She walked into the family room. "That's perfect. Thank you."

"If you just sign here"—he handed her a clipboard and a pen—"we'll be on our way."

Dani took the clipboard and signed her name. She was handed a receipt, and the delivery men left. She turned to Gabriel. "Go away. This isn't it a good time."

"Will there ever be a good time?"

"Probably not." She knew they needed to clear the air, but she didn't want to look at the past today. For the last three years, she'd forced herself to look forward and not back. Back hurt too much. Gabriel had never been a patient man, though, and he wouldn't let this go until they talked. "Are you ready to accept that I'm a member of the club?"

Gabriel shook his head. "I know how you reacted when I introduced you to kink. A leopard doesn't change its spots."

Dani rolled her eyes and moved back into the kitchen. She might as well finish emptying boxes since it didn't look like Gabriel was going to go anywhere. "No, a leopard doesn't change its spots, but it learns how to use them."

"What are you trying to tell me, Dani?"

"That I'm not the same woman I was when we were in college together." She put the plates into a cabinet. "You need to get your head around that."

"Maybe not. But I can't see you being into kink if me wanting to spank you sent us into the biggest argument we'd ever had and us breaking up."

Her gut clenched. "I can't help what you think. And you need to leave me alone." Dani turned back to the box, fighting the urge to crush the teacups between her fingers. Why should she explain everything to him now? He was the one who'd refused to listen. The room was silent, and when she turned, Gabriel was gone. She gripped the counter. Life moved on, and she had to as well. He didn't fight for her then, and apparently, he wouldn't now either. She tried to convince herself she didn't care.

It was after five when Dani finished the last box in the kitchen. She was happy but tired. And hungry. She'd eaten breakfast, but it had been so busy she totally forgot about lunch. Maybe she'd call for pizza or something to be delivered.

The doorbell rang, and she jumped. That bell was so much louder than the one in her other apartment. She walked over to the door and opened it to see Allyson, Sierra, and Crystal standing there.

"Hey, what are you guys doing here?" Max had told her not to worry about working the desk tonight; he'd help Ralph out. "And how did you get in?"

"We brought food." Each of them held up bags.

"And your neighbor saw me earlier and was happy to let us in," Allyson said.

The smell of noodles, tacos, and shrimp filled her senses, and her mouth watered.

"You are lifesavers." The women traipsed into the apartment and, within minutes, were seated around the family room, the coffee table covered with food.

"I figured you'd forget to eat." Allyson dished up some noodles into a bowl.

"I did." She used tongs to take some of the fried shrimp, then picked up a taco. "Such a mixture of food."

Sierra laughed. "We all wanted different things."

"Oh, and I almost forgot…" Crystal pulled out two six packs of beer.

Dani laughed. "Where's Tessa?"

"Damon is working at the club tonight," Crystal said.

"So are Zeke and Jordan," Allyson said.

"Yet you're here?" She tilted her head, perplexed.

"Damon and Tessa don't always get a lot of playtime together in the club, so when he's on duty, she's usually there," Sierra said.

"Oh?" Dani hadn't been around the women that much to know the ins and outs of their relationships.

"Let me clarify," Crystal said. "Tessa's mom has been visiting again. So it's really hard for them to play at home with her mother there. Tonight, she told her mom that she and Damon were going out on a date."

Dani grinned. "Now I see. Does her mother visit a lot?"

"She doesn't know the story," Allyson said, looking at her friends.

As they ate, Sierra and Crystal took turns telling Dani about Damon and Tessa's courtship and how Tessa's dad tried to blackmail her into denouncing Damon and the club. And how Tessa stood in front of town hall at a press conference and told her father to back off. She loved Damon and the people in the club. Plus, she knew her father was having an affair.

"Her mother divorced him?" Dani was astonished. She'd been so busy helping her grandparents with the business after she came home, she hadn't paid that much attention to what was going on.

"Oh yeah." Sierra waved her hand in the air. "Her mother had had enough of Tessa's father's crap. Tessa and Damon had the whole town backing them."

Dani sighed. "Now that's romance."

They all laughed and talked in general. Once they finished eating, everyone helped Dani put the leftovers away, and Crystal pulled out another six pack of beer. Dani wasn't sure she should drink another one; she'd already had two. But what did it matter? Tomorrow was Saturday.

"So you and Gabriel?" Sierra prompted with raised eyebrows.

Dani groaned; she should have known this was going to happen. "Yes. A long time ago."

"Are you going to get back together with him?" Crystal asked.

"Probably not."

The three women stared at her.

"We were college lovers, we broke up. End of story."

"But you broke up because of kink, right?" Allyson asked.

Dani closed her eyes. "That was part of it, yes."

"You're into kink now," Sierra said.

"So, what's the problem?" Crystal asked.

Dani looked at the women. "Gabriel doesn't think I belong in Wicked Sanctuary. He can't accept I'm in the lifestyle, which is weird. And there is also the fact that he's not into commitment. I'd be wasting my time."

Sierra's jaw dropped open; Crystal started coughing, and Allyson stared at her.

"I can't believe Gabriel is commitment phobic. He's such a nice guy," Sierra said.

"Being nice doesn't mean he doesn't have issues," Crystal said.

"Not into commitment? That doesn't make sense. He works with Zeke. In fact, they run the company together; how is that not commitment?" Allyson asked.

"Maybe I should say marriage commitment." Dani huffed. "How much do you ladies know about Gabriel?"

"We've all talked with him," Sierra said.

"I've had dinner with him several times, and of course,

Zeke was there. But Gabriel rarely talks about anything personal."

"That's true," Crystal said.

Dani sat back. She didn't want to betray any confidences Gabriel had shared with her. "Let's just say he didn't have good role models when he was growing up."

The women laughed.

"Not one of us did, yet we're all committed to our men," Sierra said.

"I think it's different for men," Dani said. Gabriel's parents' marriages and divorces took a toll on Gabriel. He didn't believe relationships ever lasted. She understood, or at least she thought she did. It wasn't easy. She'd had security and love her entire life. Her parents died when she was eight, but her grandparents took her in and showed her love and security.

"Let's talk about something else," Crystal said. "Tell us how you got into kink."

"San Francisco enlightened her," Allyson chimed in.

Dani grinned. "I will say once I found the right group of people, they opened my eyes to a lot." She began telling them about her adventures in San Francisco. From the private parties to the clubs to the homes she'd partied in.

* * * *

Monday morning, Gabriel pulled into the almost empty Wicked Sanctuary parking lot. Zeke had asked him to meet him at the club so they could go over all the work that had been done on the club's expansion.

He'd agreed. Gabriel didn't expect any issues. The construction team who worked on the project had been with the company for years. But last week, there'd been a couple of new guys because Riggs Construction was busy. Very busy. Heck, Gabriel had more projects than he could handle. After he was done with Zeke, he had two more meetings to go to.

"Hey, Gabriel," Zeke called.

Gabriel looked up to see Zeke waving at him from the new back wall. He strode over. "It's looking good." The expansion did look good. The walls were solid. They'd made sure of it. Since the older part of the building was concrete and rebar, they wanted this to blend in, but with better materials. More sustainable materials.

He rounded the corner and stopped. Dani was there and so was Max. "Good morning." He forced himself to sound normal. Gabriel hadn't stopped thinking about Dani since Friday. After he left her apartment, he did a lot of thinking and came to one conclusion.

He didn't want to stay away from her. If she was a changed woman who had truly gotten into kink, he wanted to be the one to show her everything he had to offer. If she was determined to be at Wicked Sanctuary, he was determined to be her Dom.

A grin tugged at his lips, thinking about the fun they'd have. She could refuse, but he didn't think she would. Because he wasn't going to be able to see her play with anyone else. While they had a history together, and a long road ahead to repair that history, he would do this right. He would show Dani he was her perfect match in the club.

"Now that Gabriel's here, we can discuss everything. Max, are there any issues?"

"None so far. The two new guys are working out just fine. We'll move the equipment away from the wall you'll be removing, so you can pull it down next week. You're progressing quite fast."

"Thank the weather for that. It's warm enough that it's moving fast. Dani?" Zeke looked at her.

Gabriel turned his attention to her. She looked sexy in her overalls. She'd put her hair into a ponytail, one he thought about tugging to see what would happen. "I've got the plants and trees on order. They'll be here in the next two weeks. My team can start putting them in." She barely glanced at him. Gabriel decided not to push it. For now, anyway.

"Good. Gabriel, there really isn't much for you to do here since the plans are already filed and approved," Zeke said.

"They are. The parking lot isn't though." He rubbed his chin. "I had pushback from the city on the expansion toward the forest." He'd seen the email this morning.

"Why? This is private land," Max said.

"I know, but they're worried about green space." He could only tell them what the email told him.

"Allyson didn't think there would be an issue," Zeke said.

"The email wasn't from her."

"That doesn't make sense," Dani spoke up. "We're replacing every tree and keeping the changes from impacting the wildlife. Do you remember who sent the email?" Dani began typing on her tablet.

"Not off the top of my head." Gabriel watched her staring down at the electronic tablet in her hand.

"Found it." She typed more. "Don't know this person. Let me reply with my drawings. Maybe then they'll understand."

"Thanks, Dani," Zeke said. "I don't want to get Allyson involved unless we have no choice."

"Dani, how many are you going to have for your job?" Max asked.

"There will be me and two of my crew. I'll forward

their background checks to you. I did them when they were hired. And since we'll be outside, there shouldn't be an issue."

Max nodded.

"Well, this was a quick meeting," Zeke said.

"Good thing." Max yawned. "I'm going to do some paperwork and go catch a nap. Dani, see you Friday night." Max waved as he left.

"I'm going to go check the dimensions on the parking lot expansion once again," Dani said and walked away. Gabriel kept his gaze on her.

"You have it bad," Zeke commented.

"What?" Gabriel shook his head, and Zeke laughed.

"Another one bites the dust."

Gabriel didn't ask Zeke what he meant. Instead, he made his way to the parking lot and straight over to Dani. "How are you?" he asked.

"Fine." She was making notes on her tablet.

He didn't like the one word answer. "Can we talk for a minute?"

Dani looked up and frowned. "I don't want to fight."

"I don't either."

She lowered her tablet and waited.

"I want us to be friends." Gabriel was aware he needed to watch how he phrased the next part so she didn't get angry or run. "I'd like us both to be able to enjoy the club."

Her eyes widened. "You're okay with me going to the club?" The disbelief in her voice almost caused him to smile. He didn't blame her. He'd been fighting it since he found out she was a member.

"I'm asking you to give us both a chance."

She stared at him with guarded eyes. "What do you mean?"

"I mean, I'd like us to play together in the club." When she started to shake her head, he captured her chin. "Don't answer now. Think about it. I'll be here Friday. That gives you all week."

"All right." Her eyes softened.

"Thank you." He breathed out a sigh of relief. Step one. Now to plan for step two.

"I need to talk with Max. I think I know why they're rejecting the plans for the parking lot. Come with me."

He took her arm and led her around the club to a back door. He held it open, motioned her to Max's office. At least she was giving them a chance, and he'd take it. Gabriel knocked on the closed office door.

"Just a second." Max's strong voice came through and then there was a loud giggle.

Gabriel glanced down at Dani, who had a wide grin on her face and pink cheeks. "Sierra's in there with him."

"I didn't think he'd cheat on Sierra," Dani said.

The door opened. "I wouldn't."

"If he did, I'd have his balls for breakfast," Sierra said.

Max gestured for them to enter his office. Sierra sat on the sofa with her legs crossed, trying to look innocent. But her lips were red, and her hair had that just-out-of-bed look. A stab of jealousy surprised Gabriel. What was it like to know someone as well as Max and Sierra knew each other? Gabriel glanced at Dani, her cute blush still coloring her cheeks. He wanted that color heightened because of him and no one else. Did that mean he wanted a relationship? No. He didn't do relationships. Did he?

"What can I do for you?" Max asked.

"I think I figured out why the city is having an issue with the parking lot," Dani said.

"That's news," Sierra said, leaning forward.

"Let's take this into the classroom. I can unroll the big plans, and you can show us." Max grabbed the large white tubes from behind his desk. Once in the classroom, Max unrolled the plans on one of the tables.

Dani leaned over, and Gabriel's dick shifted at the sight of her round ass, perfect for flogging. *Behave.* "We've extended the parking lot twenty feet out toward the trees." She pointed out the area on the plans. "I think what they're worried about is here." She slid her finger around. "This is the south end of the parking lot that leads to the main road. I'm wondering if they're worried we're going to take out the old pine trees?"

"But we're not touching them," Max said.

"No, we're not, but they could think we are based on the verbiage on the plans." She pulled up information her tablet. "It says on the accompanying paperwork: twenty feet around the entire parking lot."

"Well, damn," Gabriel muttered. "I never thought they'd think of the driveway as part of that. I can amend the report and refile. That should clear up any misunderstanding." How could he have made such a mistake?

"The other thing is to let them know we're using drought resistant plants that are more eco-friendly, and I think you'll want to install a sprinkler system in the new area."

"I didn't think of that," Max said.

"That makes a lot of sense," Sierra said. "We should put in a good watering system throughout the place."

Max groaned.

"It does make sense." Gabriel leaned over the plans. "The piping runs along this line." He ran his finger over the plans where there was a faint red line. "I bet we could tap into that easily."

"Yes, it would save time and money if we can do it without too much digging," Dani said.

"How soon can you two figure this all out and get the new plans to the city?" Max asked.

"I can reply to the email and advise that we're revising the plans and"—she glanced at Gabriel—"have the new plans to them by tomorrow afternoon?"

He nodded. "Shouldn't be a problem. I have all the electrical and plumbing on the other plans, so using those to amend the plans should be fine."

"Great. I'll leave it both to it." Max rolled up the plans, and they made their way out of the club and back to the parking lot.

"So, Friday. Do you want to come to the club together?" Gabriel asked.

"I'd rather drive myself." Dani unlocked her vehicle.

"Very well." He opened the driver's door for her.

"Thank you." Dani hopped into the driver's seat and put her bag on the passenger seat before turning back to him.

"I'll see you later." He leaned in and brushed a kiss over her cheek before stepping back and shutting the door. Dani drove off, and Gabriel took a deep breath. He needed to work on the plans for the parking lot after his meeting and forward them to Dani. Or better yet, show up with them. Exposure therapy, right? The more time she spent with him, the more she'd want to be with him. At least, that's what Gabriel was counting on.

* * * *

Dani was surprised by the kiss on her cheek. After she drove off, she placed her hand over the spot. Her skin tingled. Gabriel was pushing, asking her if she wanted to ride with him to the club on Friday. He'd surprised her by not arguing when she said she'd drive herself.

He'd asked her to play with him, but she hadn't answered. Dani didn't want any more surprises. A sub and Dom had to be upfront about terms, about hard and soft limits, and mostly about honoring safe words. They needed to discuss that before she made any decisions about playing with him.

Once back in her office, Dani went over the plans for the club once again, and forwarded her notes on to Gabriel. At one-thirty, Allyson walked into her office.

"Ready for lunch?"

"Yep." Dani grabbed her purse. "Your car or mine."

"I'll let you drive."

Dani laughed. It was rare when Allyson drove, but Dani asked anyway. She drove to Sweet & Savory. It was the best place to eat; besides, Lara owned it.

"So tell me," Allyson said after they placed their order. "What's the full story between you and Gabriel?"

Dani blew out a breath and looked at her best friend. "I told you on Saturday."

"You glossed over it. I want details."

"I didn't gloss over anything." Lucky for her it was after the lunch rush, so a good portion of the tables were empty.

"Gabriel seemed genuinely shocked when he saw you at the club, and you've told me so little about that time. So what's going on?"

Dani fiddled with the edge of her blouse. "I told you; Gabriel tried to introduce me to kink and…I freaked out."

"What?" Allyson just stared at her as if she had grown horns out of the top of her head. "You went with me to a couple of the parties in Seattle."

Dani didn't blame her. She'd gone to those parties and convinced Allyson to give them up. She was also the one who'd encouraged Allyson to get involved with Zeke.

"What did I know?" Dani said. "Even though I went to college locally, I wasn't even aware of Wicked Sanctuary or kink for that matter. Now that I think about it, Wicked Sanctuary wasn't even open yet." Dani did some quick calculations in her head. She'd been gone for three years, almost four, and Wicked Sanctuary opened five years ago. "Well, maybe they had just opened."

"Yes, hard to tell, but I don't remember you being a prude in college."

"I wasn't. Being a prude has nothing to do with it. I like sex, but when Gabriel started talking about spanking me, I kind of lost it." She really couldn't blame Gabriel for everything, but he had scared her. All she knew at the time was from what she'd read on the Internet, but now she knew it wasn't all whips and pain.

"Gabriel moved way too fast and didn't take time to explain it to you, did he?" Allyson shook her head. "Zeke took his time teaching me the right kind of kink, and it really helped."

Dani smiled. "I saw the changes in you. Zeke's been the best Dom. He did it right. The world has changed a lot in the last few years, and people are more accepting of an alternative lifestyle than they were." San Francisco had been a great place to realize that.

"Not all people." Allyson waved her hand in the air. "My parents, brothers, and my ex don't accept anything that they don't believe in."

"That's true. I'm so glad your aunt and Zeke support you." Dani was happy for her friend but, at the same time, a little envious. Yes, she had her grandparents, but she'd never discussed this type of thing with them.

"So, from what you said Saturday, in San Francisco you discovered more about the lifestyle?"

"Yes." Dani gathered her thoughts. "When I got to San Francisco, I did some research, and some of it scared me, and some of it was interesting. But in San Francisco, I didn't know anyone, and since I was working for a large company, I was pretty much just a cog in a wheel. Lucky for me, San Francisco has a pretty large kink community." A community that welcomed her with open arms even though she knew next to nothing and had several misapprehensions about the lifestyle.

"I'm not surprised."

"I was scared to death at my first munch." Dani put her elbows on the table and rested her chin on her hands. "The people at the munch noticed, but they were so nice. Several of the women rallied around me and helped ease me into the lifestyle."

"So, did you play with a Dom later?"

"Yes. This stays between you and me." Dani leaned closer to Allyson. "My Dom was older, probably close to my dad's age, if my dad was still alive. And my Dom and I never had sex."

Allyson sat back in her chair and raised her eyebrows. "No sex at all?" she whispered.

"None at all. He and I played together, and he taught me about the lifestyle. He showed me being a submissive wasn't a bad thing, but having sex wasn't part of our deal."

"I can't imagine playing with Zeke and not having sex later."

"Of course you can't. You love Zeke." Dani sat back in her own chair and gave a small smile. "The love between my Dom and I was really that of a mentor/mentee type of thing. We weren't in love, and neither of us was interested in sex with the other."

"I guess it's a good way to learn."

"It was for me. It opened my eyes to what the lifestyle was about."

"That all makes sense, but that was four years ago. You've changed, and I'm pretty sure Gabriel's changed," Allyson said.

"I'm not so sure how much he's changed." Dani rested her chin on her palm. "I honestly don't know what to do. Gabriel says he wants us to be friends, but with so much history behind us, I'm not sure we can be."

"You are not your past."

Dani's stomach clenched. "That's not going to be easy. Plus, I'm not sure how much Gabriel will really listen to me." She wanted a long-term relationship, one like her grandparents. If experience was any indication, Gabriel would never agree to that. His parents had taught him marriage was a convenience, like a tissue. Once used, throw it away and get a new one.

"If this is important to him, he'll listen."

They sat in silence for a few minutes. "I'm not sure," Dani said. "He does want to play with me in the club."

"That's an interesting turn of events. Just talk to him and let him talk to you. Communication is so important in the lifestyle."

Dani laughed. "Don't I know it." She glanced up as one of the staff brought their food. She needed to talk with Gabriel and get him to understand how she came to like kink and why she needed it. But would he listen to her? Really listen? He had some preconceived notions about her and kink, and Dani wasn't confident he could move past them.

Chapter 3

Dani kicked off her shoes as her doorbell rang Thursday night. She frowned. The reason she'd moved into this apartment was because of the security door. Padding to the door, she looked out the peep hole.

Gabriel. She was surprised to see him there. She opened her door, her heart pounding. "How did you get in?"

He stood there with a big grin on his face, a large bag dangling from his fingers and holding a pizza box. "Hello to you too." He jerked his head. "Your neighbor let me in when she saw the pizza box, and she is watching and waiting. She told me she'd call 911 if you slammed the door in my face."

Dani poked her head out to see Mrs. Bower standing by the security door with her cell phone in her hand. "He said he wanted to surprise you with dinner," the woman announced.

"Thank you, Mrs. Bower," she called back. "Come in." Dani stepped back so Gabriel could walk in.

"Peace offering." He gestured to the pizza box and the large bag.

"I'd say get lost, but I missed lunch, and that smells delicious." The scent of pizza dough, tomato sauce, cheese, and bacon tickled her nose. Her stomach growled. She shut the door. "Put everything on the table, and I'll grab plates and stuff. What do you want to drink?"

"I brought drinks. And salad." She watched him move to the small table. Dani almost moaned. The jeans he wore cupped his ass just right. He glanced over his shoulder, so she ducked her head and made a beeline for the kitchen.

"You always did love my ass." Gabriel's laughter floated through the air, and her nerve endings came alive. Maybe this was a chance for her and Gabriel to be friends. She grabbed plates, bowls, utensils, glasses, and napkins.

Gabriel was unloading the bag. The pizza sat in the middle of the table. "I also brought garlic bread and beer." He finished placing everything on the table.

"My hero." Dani smiled at him. He knew exactly what she liked.

He grinned. "I like being called a hero. I do have one more thing I think you'll like." He reached into the bag. Dani spied the container and squealed.

"Oh. My. God. Gimme, gimme, gimme." Her mouth watered for that gooey chocolatey nutty piece of heaven.

"Dinner first, then dessert." He placed the cake back in the bag.

"Spoilsport." Dani was laughing as she said it. This reminded her of them together in college. Gabriel would always bring her dessert but made sure she ate dinner first. It was a happy memory. A good memory.

Gabriel pulled out one of the chairs, and Dani sat. Always a gentleman. He opened her beer and then the pizza box. "Dig in."

She didn't need to be told twice. She put two slices of pizza on her plate, added salad to her bowl and dug in. She would get to the garlic bread in a few minutes. She sighed as the cheese, tangy sauce, and dough hit her tongue.

When she paused to take a sip of her beer, she noticed Gabriel watched her. She tilted her head. "Do I have sauce on my face?" She grabbed a napkin and wiped it over her lips. It came away clean.

"I love the way you enjoy food. I've missed that."

Dani put her napkin down. "I know I left abruptly, and I'm sorry I did that."

"It wasn't all your fault. Let's finish eating and then talk."

She nodded. He seemed willing to talk, so maybe that meant he would listen. If they could clear the air enough for them to be friends, all would be good. After another ten minutes, Dani sat back in her chair.

"Oh my God, as much as I want to eat that cake now, if I take another bite of anything, I'm going to explode."

"It will keep." He pulled it out of the bag. "It does need to go in the fridge."

"I'll take care of it." Dani stood and piled the salad container on top of the nearly empty pizza box along with the cake and carried it all into the kitchen.

Gabriel followed with the garlic bread and their plates. "Do you want to take some of the leftovers home?" She pulled out a container for the salad.

"No, you can keep them." He dropped the garlic bread on the counter and watched while she made short work of wrapping up everything and putting it into the fridge. She gave the cake a longing look before she shut the door.

"Shall we sit down and talk?" He grasped her by the elbow, and they walked out of the kitchen.

"Yes." Though part of her wanted to tell him she was tired, and they could talk another night. They needed to talk. "So you're an architect with Zeke's company."

"Yes. I put my degree to good use, as you did." He turned toward her, putting his arm over the back of the sofa. "Why didn't you come and see me right after you got back?"

"There was so much going on at first." She rubbed her forehead. "When Gran called me to say Pop had a heart attack, I couldn't think of anything but getting back here to help them. Thankfully, it wasn't bad, although he's still weak, even after a year."

"You could've called me. I dropped by the hospital and at your grandparents' home to check in with them but never saw you."

Dani dipped her head as her cheeks heated. "Usually, when you came to the hospital, I had run home to shower and change or get something to eat." She looked at Gabriel, wanting honesty between them. "I never said thank you for what you did for my grandparents."

"And after your grandfather was able to go home, you decided to stay?"

"I had to go back to San Francisco for a few days." That had been fun. Not. Her boss hadn't been happy with her taking several weeks off, and to be honest, at that point, she hadn't cared. The man had never seen her as more than a glorified assistant anyway. "I had to give my notice, pack up my apartment, and move back here."

"No hesitation in leaving San Francisco? Did you leave a trail of broken hearts?"

Her lips twitched. "No broken hearts and I wasn't about to let the family landscaping business die or be sold." Her family needed her, and that was all that mattered.

"I'm glad you came home." His fingers drummed against the back of the sofa. "Care to explain about Wicked Sanctuary."

She bit her lip. "As I said, things change."

"Sweetheart, you freaked out when I tried to introduce you to kink." He leaned forward. "Even though we didn't talk about it afterward, you started to drift away. I thought maybe after graduation, we might revisit kink, but you left."

Her gut clenched. "I'm sorry." What else could she say? "I was in a bad place mentally. I didn't know anything about kink at that time, and yes, you frightened me." She made a quick decision on what to tell him. "Kink was only part of the issue that caused me to withdraw. I was so stressed about finals."

"That's why I thought some kink might help you relax."

She shook her head. "It was a bad time to spring it on me." There were some things she wasn't ready to tell him yet. "We stopped communicating with each other," she said.

"I agree. I shut down."

Dani was shocked by the admission. The old Gabriel never would have said that. But he wasn't to blame for everything. "I have to take some responsibility as well. You wouldn't listen to me when I tried to explain things to you. I…" She didn't know what else to say.

"I get it. Now what?" He spread his hands out in front of him.

She sat, thinking for a moment. "Do you think we can be friends?" They were bound to see each other. While she'd avoided running into him since she got home, after the bookstore, the Band-Aid had been ripped off. She wasn't going to avoid him anymore.

"I'd like us to be friends, but I'm also not sure about you playing at Wicked Sanctuary."

She yawned. The early day was catching up with her.

"You're tired." He reached out and took her hand. "We do need to talk about why you're at the club, but I want you well rested when we have the talk. How about lunch tomorrow?"

There was a twinge of frustration in his voice, and she bit her lip. She didn't mean to do this to him, but she wasn't going to give up something that made her happy. "I can do that."

His eyes brightened. "Sweet & Savory at eleven. I'll get us a table in the back."

"All right." Another yawn escaped her lips. "Sorry, I was up at four."

"It's okay." Gabriel stood and helped her to her feet. When they reached her apartment door, he opened it. "Lock it behind me."

"Bossy."

"You bet I am." He leaned down and brushed a soft kiss over her lips, stepped through the threshold, and shut the door.

Dani locked it, but instead of moving away, she laid her palms against the door as if she could see feel Gabriel's presence. Would he be able to accept she was now into kink? And how would he feel when she eventually told him why she'd pulled away.

She pushed away from the door, turned off the lights, and made her way into her bedroom. Tears threated to spill over. She cried enough all those years ago. Even now, she felt as if a part of her was missing. A part she could never get back. She also worried Gabriel would never forgive her for what happened.

* * * *

Dani stepped into Sweet & Savory the next day and looked around for Gabriel. "He's in the new area," Lara said.

"Thanks." Dani fought against the embarrassment of Lara knowing who she was looking for. There was nothing to be self-conscious about. She walked into the new section of the café. It was great that Lara had been able to expand her business.

Gabriel stood the moment he saw her. "Hey, Dani," he said, pulling out a chair for her.

"Gabriel." She sat. These little gentlemanly things Gabriel did warmed her heart. She'd forgotten how considerate he could be.

"What would you like to eat?" he asked as he hovered next to her.

"How about a bowl of broccoli cheddar soup, the veggie wrap, a piece of my favorite cake, and iced tea, please."

"Coming right up." Gabriel went to order, and Dani sat back in her chair. She was a little tired today, but that was because her mind wouldn't shut down last night. She kept thinking about her and Gabriel.

A number was deposited at the end of the table as Gabriel sat down across from her. "Drinks will be here shortly."

Dani nodded. She didn't know what to say.

"Did you sleep last night?" Gabriel asked.

"Not really."

"Me either."

"Really?" That surprised her. When they were together, he'd slept like a log.

"Yes." He glanced out the window and back at her. "I've missed you, Dani."

"We just saw each other last night."

"That's not what I meant."

Lara walked up to the table and set their drinks down. "Dani, you want your soup and wrap together?"

"Yes, that's fine."

Lara nodded and left. Dani waited for Gabriel to continue.

"I've missed being with you," he said.

His admission took her back. "You seemed okay when we broke up."

"I wasn't okay." He drummed his fingers on the table. A nervous habit he had. She hid a smile. "I realized the day after graduation that I wanted to make things work between us, but you'd already left for San Francisco."

Shock ran through her veins. "You wanted to make it work?" Did he even realize what he was saying? "It wasn't going to work. We wanted different things."

"Did we?" He reached across the table and placed his hand over hers.

The warmth of his skin seeped into hers. "We did." She didn't pull away. "I wanted commitment, and you didn't."

"That didn't mean we couldn't stay together. You could have gone to work with your grandfather."

"And where would that have led us?" She'd thought about it before she accepted the offer with the company in San Francisco. But, at the time, it was better for her to get away from Pleasant Valley and Gabriel.

"We would have made it work."

"Oh, Gabriel," she whispered. "We were young, maybe too young. Both of us had just graduated with our degrees."

"It was only four years ago."

"A lifetime." From the way he looked at her, he didn't fully understand. "We needed time away from each other. We dated exclusively the last two years in college."

"Are you saying you wanted to date other men?" He pulled his hand back.

"No. What I'm saying is, we needed time apart to grow into the people we were meant to be." It seemed like she'd lived a lifetime in the past four years. San Francisco, learning about kink, her grandfather's heart attack, coming home, seeing Gabriel again.

"I…" He broke off as Lara arrived at their table with the food. She set it down and left. "Eat and then we'll talk."

Dani looked down at her food, her appetite gone. "I want to get this out. Why do you think things would have been different if we'd stayed together?" She really wanted to know what he was thinking.

"Because we were good together. I sprang kink on you, and that's my bad. But we could have made a go of things."

"If you felt that way, why didn't you contact me in San Francisco? My grandparents knew where I was."

Gabriel stiffened. "I was angry you left."

"Right. Can't you see, Gabriel, if we'd stayed together, it would have reinforced your opinion about marriage."

He froze. "You know why I have that opinion."

"Yes, but I'm not your mother, and you're not your father."

"You don't know that." He pushed his food away.

"No, I don't." She'd have to get Lara to wrap up everything to go. "I do know I needed time to get my head on straight and stretch my wings."

"San Francisco did that for you?" His features were closed.

"Yes." How could she make him understand. "It wasn't that I wanted to date other men. I needed to prove to myself I could stand on my own two feet." It was more than that, but she wouldn't talk to him about it. Gabriel would take it the wrong way.

"What about kink?"

"That was an accident." Her lips turned up. "I happened to be talking with two of the other women who worked in the landscaping company. We got to chatting, and at one point, kink came up. It had been over a year since we'd been together, so I talked with them. They took me to my first munch."

"And you liked it?"

"I was scared to death, but they introduced me around, and I met some good people."

"Max mentioned you went through training and the classes at the club." His fingers began drumming against the table once again.

"Yes. Max was willing to waive them, but I told him not to."

"Why?"

Dani pulled her soup bowl close and spooned some into her mouth. Ah, not to hot, not too cold. She did this to give herself a minute to gather her thoughts, but also because she was getting hungry. After a few more bites, she looked at him. "Because I wanted to know how Max ran his club."

"That makes sense. I understand Bennett was your training Dom."

"He was." She smiled, thinking about the blond-haired, baby-faced Dom. "Bennett is nice and sweet. He guided me through the classes and helped me in the club."

"Did you sleep with him?"

Her head jerked up, and she glared at Gabriel. "No, and if this is how this discussion is going to go—" She pushed back her chair.

"No." Gabriel stood up. "I'm sorry; that was uncalled for. Please sit back down."

The pain in his eyes struck a nerve, and she retook her seat.

"Thank you," he said.

"For the record, Bennett and I didn't play together outside of the club."

"But he was your trainer?" The astonishment in his voice was loud and clear.

"He was. That's all he was." Dani finished her soup before it got ice cold. "Bennett is sweet and helped me a lot, but he's not my boyfriend. Not that I need to explain myself to you. I don't sleep around like your mother did. When I'm with someone, there's no one else. You should already know that about me."

"I didn't say you were like her."

"Right." Would he ever understand she wasn't going to jump from man to man. Just like he didn't jump from woman to woman, at least not that she knew of.

"Everything okay?" Lara asked.

"Fine," Gabriel snapped.

Dani shook her head. "We're good, Lara, but I think we might need the food to go."

"Sure. No problem." Lara picked up Dani's wrap and Gabriel's sandwich. "I'll get these wrapped up along with dessert."

"We still need to talk," Gabriel said.

"Not until you get it through your thick skull that I'm not like your mother and never will be."

"Dani…" he started.

She held up her hand. "I understand your parents influenced you a lot when it comes to relationships. I get it. But I'm not willing to sit here and discuss my life with you unless you're willing to make an effort."

"I'm the one who asked you here."

"You did. But I'm seeing you haven't changed much. I have." She took a breath as Lara arrived with their food in bags. "Thank you for lunch, but think about what I said before you contact me again." Dani stood and picked up her bag. "Good food, Lara." She walked out, her heart pounding and a lead ball in her belly.

* * * *

Gabriel watched Dani walk out, frozen in his seat. What the hell had just happened? He glanced up at Lara. "Sorry, Dani and I seem to cross wires every time."

"Maybe you should listen to what she's really trying to say." Lara turned and walked away.

Gabriel picked up his bag, walked into the main part of the café, and dropped some money in the tip jar before going out to his vehicle. Now what? He wasn't going to go to the club tonight. No, he wasn't ready to see Dani there and possibly playing with another Dom.

He slammed the door of his SUV. He'd call Zeke, but he'd taken Allyson, her aunt, and his mother to go see a play in Seattle. There was only one thing he could do. That was work. He'd put Dani out of his mind until he could talk with Zeke.

* * * *

Gabriel knocked on the door of Wicked Sanctuary, and it was pulled open. "Good to see you, Gabriel," Jordan said. "Zeke commented you'd be here."

"Yeah." Gabriel had briefly talked to Zeke yesterday afternoon, and Zeke told him about the Dom meeting today and that he should come.

"We're all in back in the temp classroom." Jordan motioned down the hall.

Gabriel followed Jordan, and when he stepped into the room, he was glad to see most of the Wicked Sanctuary Doms there. Zeke waved him to a seat next to him. Gabriel sat down.

"I didn't expect so many to be here," Gabriel said

softly.

"It's actually a good group," Zeke said.

"It's two, so let's start," Max said. "Anyone want to pipe up with action items?"

For the next two hours, they talked about the subs, items Doms were unsure about, and gave advice. Not that Gabriel had much advice, but now he knew why Zeke encouraged him to come. The Doms gave him some insight on things he'd never thought about.

The meeting broke up, and he walked with Zeke out to the parking lot. "You okay, buddy?" Zeke asked.

"Yeah." Gabriel leaned against his vehicle. "Actually, no. Dani and I can't seem to see eye to eye right now."

"Ah. That explains the lengthy phone call Allyson had yesterday."

"I'm sorry." Gabriel didn't know what else to say.

"I only know what you've told me about the history between you and Dani, but I do know she's not afraid of kink. If you want to be her Dom in the club, you'll need to prove to her you know that as well."

"My head is aware, but the gut clenches every time."

"Why is that?"

"I told you how she reacted." He ran his hand through his hair.

"Any woman would have reacted that way. You brought up spanking out of the blue; you said yourself she was stressed about finals. Now think how you would feel if someone, while you were super stressed, brought up, let's say bloodletting."

Gabriel scrunched up his face. "Ugh."

"Exactly. I know it's hard, but put yourself in Dani's shoes back when you sprang kink on her."

"Well, damn." It hit him like a ton of bricks. What a

selfish ass he'd been. He not only sprang it on her, he didn't do much in the way of explaining. Why hadn't he'd seen it before? Because he was too wrapped up in himself and wasn't taking Dani's feelings into consideration. That's why.

"Now what are you going to do?" Zeke asked.

"Apologize, but it's more than that."

"I see. Want to go get a beer and chat more?" Zeke asked.

"Not today." He needed to wrap his head around a few things first. "Thanks. You've helped me." Gabriel clapped Zeke on the shoulder.

"See you tomorrow; we've got a meeting at ten with the Stamfords."

"Yep, it's on my calendar." Gabriel climbed into his SUV. He had some thinking to do and some apologizing.

* * * *

Dani finished planting the last of the bushes around the new library. She was happy with them. "They look nice." Dani turned to see Tessa standing behind her.

"Hi, Tessa." She dusted her hands off, stood, and brushed the dirt off her knee pads. "I'm glad you like them."

"They don't look drought resistant."

"They're not supposed to. When Zeke brought me in to do the landscaping, and with the permission of the county, we installed a rainwater system."

"Is that the big white thing in the back?"

"Yep. It will collect the rainwater to be used for irrigation and other non-drinkable things. It will help keep the costs down for the library and also help the environment."

"I love it." Tessa gave her a big smile.

"Was there something else?" She was a little surprised to see Tessa.

"I wanted to check in with you. You were quiet at the subs' meeting yesterday."

Dani's lips turned up. "I have a lot on my mind."

"I bet. Plus, we can be a noisy bunch when we get together. Allyson just wanted to make sure—" She broke off.

"Make sure I'm okay?" Dani loved her best friend. She was worried when Dani refused to play on Friday night and left right after her shift.

"Yes. We were all a little worried."

"I'm okay." Was she? Well, as okay as she could be. She still hadn't come to any decisions about Gabriel. Really, there wasn't much for her to decide. The ball was in his court now.

"I don't mean to pry." Tessa glanced down at her feet.

"It's okay." And it was. This was something Dani had missed while she was in San Francisco—having girl friends who cared. Yes, she had friends in the lifestyle, but she only saw them when she went out with them. Here was different. "I'm glad I have friends to check on me."

Tessa blew out a breath. "Thank you. Allyson seemed concerned, and in turn, that made us all concerned."

"You are all the best. You welcomed me into Wicked Sanctuary even though I'm still pretty much a novice."

"Of course we did. We've all been there. It's almost lunch time; do you want to grab a bite to eat? And I'll tell you about Damon's and my courtship. It was crazy."

"I heard about what your father did. I'm sorry."

Tessa laughed. "I'm not. It got my mother out of a bad relationship, and he finally realized that I wasn't going to bow down to his wishes. Lunch?"

"Yes, let's." Dani liked Tessa, and she wanted to spend more time with her.

* * * *

Dani laughed so hard she had tears running down her face. "Oh my God, Damon makes adult toys, and your father threatened to out him?"

"He did. The thing is, Damon isn't ashamed of what he does."

"Nor should he be." Dani loved how open Tessa was, not that the others weren't, but she'd really only had one best friend in her life, and that was Allyson.

"When it all went public, Damon and I didn't care about us, but we were worried about the club. Max and Jordan let us know in no uncertain terms that the club would be just fine."

"It looks that way. I know I haven't been a member long, but business has picked up. Even I can tell that."

"Yes, I can't wait for the new expansion to open." Tessa sat back in her seat. "So you and Gabriel were lovers in college."

Dani coughed. "Yes."

"Then why is he moping around, and why didn't you stay on Saturday night."

"Gabriel is moping?" That was news to her.

"According to Jordan, he's like a bear pulled out of hibernation before he was ready."

Dani could picture Gabriel's expression. "It's a long story."

"Give me the highlights."

"We were lovers in college, had a bad break up; I went to San Francisco, and now I'm back."

"There's more than that."

"A bit. Let's just say my introduction to kink was done

poorly."

"But you're into it now."

Dani nodded. "While I was in San Francisco, I learned about the lifestyle. I enjoy certain aspects of it."

Tessa frowned. "It doesn't sound like you had a good experience in the Bay Area."

"It wasn't bad. Nothing like Allyson's, but Wicked Sanctuary is so different. Safe. Comfortable."

"It is." Tessa beamed. "Max has made sure there is a safe place for subs and Doms alike. Even through all the crap with my father, Max kept the club secure."

"I noticed security is big here. It was one of the reasons I volunteered to help Ralph."

"Once the upgrades are finished, there will be even more security measures. A few people have slipped through, but Max is constantly working to make sure everyone is safe and happy."

"It's like a small family."

"It is. An extended family where if you need anything, ask. We'll be there for you."

Dani swallowed. "That's nice."

"Which brings me to the point of this lunch." Tessa grinned. "Do you need help bringing Gabriel to heel?"

"What?" Dani sputtered.

"Hey, we subs know how to get our Doms to behave the way we want. It just takes cunning and time."

Dani shook her head. "No, I don't need anything like that. Gabriel has issues with commitment. He needs to work those out before we can even think about our relationship or the club."

Tessa tilted her head. "I see. Have you always known this, or is it something new?"

"I've known it for a while."

"All right, I'll let it be. But honestly, if you need any help, let us know. We have our evil ways."

* * * *

Friday evening, Dani sat in the reception area with Ralph. After her lunch with Tessa on Monday, she'd had phone calls from Sierra and Crystal. Then yesterday, Lara had chatted with her at the café.

Allyson had called her this morning to make sure she was coming to the club tonight. She was thinking of staying tonight. She might not play, but she wanted to be around her friends.

"Dani, can I see you for a minute, please?" Max was standing next to her.

"I can handle things. Shut down and talk with Max," Ralph offered.

"Okay." Her stomach churned as she shut down her computer. What did Max want? She followed him down the hall and into the temporary classroom.

"Please stop looking like a scolded puppy." Max gestured for her to take a seat.

"Sorry, Master Max." Dani sat and folded her hands into her lap.

"Drop the Master." Max sat down across from her with his knees almost touching hers. "You know you can tell me anything, right?"

"Yes, Mas…Max."

"Okay. Are you happy here, Dani?"

"Yes, of course I am." What was he asking? Did she seem that unhappy?

"There is no 'of course' about it. May I?" He gestured to her hands, and she nodded. Max picked up her hands in his. "I want to be sure of your well-being."

"I'm fine. Gabriel and I have some issues to work out,

but it has nothing to do with the club."

"Good." He squeezed her hands. "I'm very pleased with your work with Ralph."

"Do I hear a *but*?"

Max shook his head. "No buts. As you know, I'm expanding the club, and with that, comes more work and security."

Dani nodded; Tessa had told her about it.

"I didn't want to assume you'd keep working at the desk with Ralph."

"Oh. I don't mind if you want me to continue."

"That means you might be at the desk with Ralph later or even by yourself for a while. I'm having new security cameras installed, and Ralph's attention will be on them at times."

"I can handle it." She could.

"Yes, you can. There's going to be a new computer system as well. So with all that, I wanted you to know that what you're doing has become a paid position."

Dani opened her mouth, but Max just stared at her, and she stayed quiet.

"Don't argue, but because I suspect you're like others here, the payment will be in the form of your yearly dues and nightly costs."

"That's very generous of you." It was. The yearly dues were high.

"I want you to be happy. You and Ralph work well together. I'll also be asking for another sub or two to help out when you're not available because I don't expect you to be here every night."

"I only work Fridays and Saturdays." It beat sitting at home.

"Yes, but there may be a time when you need a night

off or are sick. I'd rather be prepared."

"That works." Max still held her hands, so she wondered if there was something else. "Is there something more?"

Max nodded. "Gabriel."

Dani shook her head. "Gabriel is fine." She wouldn't deny Gabriel time in the club—she could deal. The question was could he.

"Are you two on speaking terms?"

"I think so." Were they? She hadn't talked to him since last Saturday, and she hadn't expected to. She'd pretty much thrown the ball in his court. It was time for him to decide what he wanted.

"All right. I won't meddle, but I can't guarantee Sierra and the others won't."

Dani grinned. "It's fine, Max."

"Good." He squeezed her hands again and released her. "I'll let you know when the training on the new system will happen. I'm afraid it will be on a Saturday or Sunday."

"I can work with that." Max stood, and she followed suit.

"Go into the club so Sierra doesn't think I killed you." He grinned.

Dani slipped out of the classroom and into the club. Leather, pine, and—her nose wrinkled—sweat.

"There she is," Sierra said, entwining her arm with Dani's. "We were beginning to worry."

"I'm good." They walked over to the sub area. A sense of peace filled her. Yes, she enjoyed being at the club.

* * * *

It was almost ten when Gabriel walked into Wicked Sanctuary. He'd debated with himself for the past few hours whether this was a good idea. He signed in and went to put his things in a locker.

He didn't need to change; he wasn't planning on playing, so he left his shirt on, and his pants were fine. He walked into the club. He caught the beat of the music and took in a slow, deep breath and let it out.

Here he could let go of everything. Forget about work and his parents. He needed this. Sliding up to the bar, he sat on one of the stools and looked around. Jordan had Crystal tied up on one of the bondage tables. Damon and Tessa were at a St. Andrew's cross, and Rose and Oliver were at the spanking horse. They looked good together. It was amazing what the right Dom did for Rose. And the right sub; Oliver never looked so happy. He grinned as his gaze turned to the sub area.

There she was. Dani was sitting with Allyson and Sage. He hadn't seen Sage in a while. After the dust up at the end of last year with Brady's family, she and Brady had kept a low profile. He was glad to see her here.

He slipped off the stool and walked over to where Dani sat.

"Gabriel," Sage said, jumping up. "Okay to hug?"

"Of course." He held his arms open.

Sage gave him a big hug before stepping back. "How are you doing?"

"All right." He glanced at Dani and Allyson. "Evening, ladies."

Dani kept her gaze on him, and she stood. "I'm going to call it a night."

Allyson's face fell, but she nodded. "I'll walk you out."

"Dani," Gabriel started.

Still at Gabe's side, Sage whispered, "Not tonight."

"Have a good evening, Sage, Gabriel," Dani said before walking away.

Gabriel watched her walk across the floor with Allyson at her side. How was he going to make it up to Dani if she wouldn't even talk to him?

"Looks like you messed up good," Sage remarked, gesturing to the quiet area of the club.

"I can't argue that." Together, they found an empty sofa and sat down. "How have you been, Sage?"

"Fine. Life has been a little busy." Sage eyed him up and down. "You're not a stupid man, so what is going on that Dani is practically ignoring you?"

While he'd talked some of this out with Zeke, maybe having a woman's opinion would help. A woman and a Dominant. "We were lovers in college. I tried to introduce kink, and she freaked out. I didn't do it right back then. I know that now. We graduated and went our separate ways."

Sage frowned. "That doesn't sound like the Dani I've seen." She rubbed her fingers over her chin. "But it also doesn't explain why she won't talk to you now."

Gabriel had figured out the answer, just like he'd known the answer in college. "Commitment."

"Ah, as in she wants it or doesn't?"

"She wants it from me." Gabriel looked at Sage. "In my experience growing up—and as an adult—showing commitment doesn't mean anything. My dad is on his fifth marriage and my mother on her fourth."

"Well, aren't they a pair? That doesn't mean you can't commit to one woman."

"You're right, but the fear is there. I don't want to hurt Dani."

"And aren't you hurting her right now?"

"What?" Shock went through his veins. "The last thing I want is to hurt her."

"You're doing it without even trying. Let me tell you

about the Dani I see. She's a brave woman who is embracing her sensuality, and she loves her job and her family. She's loyal to her friends and enjoys coming to the club to relax."

"I didn't even know she was a member until a few weeks ago. Hell, she's kept her distance since she came home. It's apparent she doesn't want to be around me."

"Yet you're both moping over each other." Sage sighed. "Listen, sometimes you need to take the reins, so to speak, but other times, you need to be gentle and easy going."

"Nothing is easy with Dani."

"Are you sure about that?"

Gabriel opened his mouth and shut it. They got along the night they had pizza…up to a point. Even during the lunch at Sweet & Savory. It was when things got a little too personal, a little too emotional that they had issues. Correction. He had issues, and she reacted to that. Oh yes, now he could see it. Well, damn.

"Thanks, Sage." He leaned toward her. "May I?" She nodded, and he kissed her cheek. "You've been a big help." Gabriel stood. While Dani might have left, he could still talk with Allyson and some of the other subs. He had some things to figure out and quick.

Chapter 4

Dani stared at her phone screen Monday morning. Unknown number. Not unusual. "Hello."

"Hi, Dani, Gabriel here, in case you didn't know by the sound of my voice."

The laughter in his voice was nice. It had been a while since she'd heard him sound so carefree.

"What can I do for you?"

"I wanted to invite you to dinner Thursday night."

"Is that a good idea? Our last couple of meals didn't turn out so well." She shifted from one foot to the other.

"Please." When she stayed silent, he continued. "This will be the last one if you tell me to leave you alone."

Her heart stopped. Did she really want him to leave her alone? She wasn't sure. "All right." She had trouble resisting Gabriel. Always had. Plus, she needed to clear the air with him one last time before she totally gave up on a relationship with him.

"Fantastic. I'll pick you up at six."

"I'd rather drive myself." In case she needed a quick getaway.

"Please, let me drive you."

Two pleases in the same conversation. "All right, but if I say I want to go home, you'll take me, or I can get a rideshare, right?"

"I will. I promise."

Her heart pounded, but this felt right. "Okay. Thursday at six."

"You won't regret it."

The line went dead, and Dani just stared at her phone. To cover any possibility, she checked her rideshare app to make sure it was up-to-date. Why did she have a feeling Gabriel had something up his sleeve?

* * * *

Dani paced around her apartment Thursday evening. It was five fifty-five. She was ready. Gabriel hadn't mentioned where they were going, and since it was such a nice evening, she opted for a sun dress and sandals.

The intercom buzzed. "Yes."

"Hey, Dani. I'm here."

"Be right there." She picked up her purse and stepped outside her apartment. She locked the door and made her way down the hallway. Gabriel was standing patiently outside the security door.

"You look fantastic," he said when she opened the door.

"Thank you." She took in his freshly pressed black pants and open neck polo shirt. "You look good too."

"I appreciate that." Gabriel held out his arm, and she placed hers through his. He guided her to his SUV. "I made reservations at the steak house; I hope that's okay?" he asked as he pulled out of the parking spot.

"It's fine." Why was she so nervous? It wasn't like she hadn't been out with Gabriel before. The ride to the restaurant was quiet.

"Will you tell me more about your life in San Francisco?" Gabriel asked after they ordered their food.

She hesitated for a moment, but realized she wanted him to understand about how she'd changed. "Sure." Dani told Gabriel about her life in San Francisco and how she discovered kink. He would stop her at times and ask questions. He seemed surprised when she told him there had been no sex between her and her Dom.

In turn, she asked him about becoming part of Zeke's construction company and how he liked his job. It was almost like a first date.

Food arrived. They ate and chatted about their friends and how much Pleasant Valley had changed. Gabriel asked about the landscaping business, and Dani was happy that the company was doing so great. With all the landscaping around the club and other jobs, she barely kept up.

Their empty plates were taken away. "This was nice," she said.

"Yes." Gabriel started to drum his finger on the table, but stopped the second he realized what he was doing.

Dani hid a grin.

"I think you understand I want us to be more than just friends."

She swallowed as she tensed up. "Yes, but I'm not sure we can be."

"I'd like to try if you're willing."

There was something in his expression. Hope, combined with a little bit of fear. "You said if?"

"Kink is all about consent. It's come to my attention that I never really asked you. That was my mistake, and I won't break the consent convention again. It's important to me and to the lifestyle."

Dani tilted her head and stared at him. "What changed?" Something had to have happened for him to come to this revelation.

"I talked with some of the other Doms. I approached you the wrong way all those years ago. I can see that now. You had a right to be angry with me. I made the same mistake a few weeks ago. I will do better."

The sincerity in his voice caused excitement to shimmer through her veins. He was taking the first step. "What are you proposing?"

"Will you allow me to be your Dom?"

Dani tilted her head. The request didn't surprise her, but she wasn't sure it would work out. However, if she didn't try, she would never know. "I have some conditions."

He spread his hands out in front of him on the table. "Go for it."

"Dom in the club is acceptable."

"What about in the bedroom?"

"Who says I'm going to be in your bedroom?" she asked.

Gabriel laughed. Waves of contentment slid over Dani's skin like a soft blanket.

"We're explosive together. I can all but guarantee there's going to be sex between us."

Instead of making her back away, his announcement made her body light up like a Christmas tree, all tingling and excited. "All right, but we make the decision together at the time it happens."

"Agreed." He held his hand out, palm up. She slipped her hand into his. "Will you tell me what your hard limits are?"

"It would probably be easier to tell you what I will do rather than what I won't."

"Does kink still scare you on some level?" Gabriel shifted closer to her.

"Not really. There are just a lot of things I don't want to try." Although part of her began to wonder if doing some of those things with Gabriel would be different than what she'd watched in the clubs.

"All right. Tell me what you will do."

"Bondage, toys, light flogging, and certain paddles."

"That's pretty limited." He ran his finger over her warm cheek. "Do you mind if I read your questionnaire?"

"Not at all. Even though I was in the kink community in San Francisco, I'm really still a novice. Max insisted I wear a pink and white wristband."

"Max is a good judge. He's right. You may feel like you're a novice, but compared to a new sub, you're not."

He studied her for a minute. "Going forward, I want you to understand if you accept me as your Dom, we're going see each other outside the club. Exclusively."

"What do you mean by that?" Dani didn't pull her hand back, and his fingers tightened around hers.

"I mean..." He hesitated, and Dani wondered what that meant. "I'm going to lay this out. I really want you to say yes to me being your Dom. Once I have your agreement, it means we will see each other in the club and outside the club. And we'll talk about each aspect and any changes. So maybe we won't make as many mistakes."

Dani tilted her head and stared at him. "Neither one of us is perfect."

"You're right about half of that, anyhow. I'm not perfect."

Dani's heart melted. Gabriel's words told her how much he'd thought about this. They both had. This time, they would communicate better. "It wasn't all your fault." She'd closed down on him. Maybe she should start paying more attention to her attitude. "I haven't been exactly forthcoming."

"I get it." He squeezed her fingers again. "You mentioned to me you were stressed those last few months we were together. Can you talk to me about it?"

She shook her head. "It's not something I'm ready to discuss. My regret is that I stopped talking to you. We graduated, and I couldn't see anything improving, so I took the job in San Francisco. By the time I realized my reaction was over the top, the damage was done, and we'd both moved on."

"You could've called me, texted me, or even emailed me."

The confusion in his eyes tugged at her guilt. She wasn't ready to discuss all her secrets. "It wasn't about you. I needed to deal with my situation, and I did." Maybe not the way she should have. It took a year of counseling for her to realize that what happened was not her fault, and even if she had told Gabriel, there was nothing he could have done.

"I believe one of the first things we need to do is to learn to trust each other again."

Dani sucked in a breath. He wasn't wrong. Somewhere along the line in the relationship, they had lost their trust of each other. She didn't want that to happen again. "I agree. I'd like to read your club questionnaire." That would give her some more insight to him.

"I expect nothing less. And I'll read yours. Let me go outside to call Max and see what's the best time for us to go to the club and read them. Does that work for you?"

"Yes."

"Be right back." Gabriel released her hand and stood. She watched him walk away and admired the way his pants gripped his ass. She groaned and smiled, then ordered coffee for both of them when the waiter walked up to the table.

"Coffee, thanks." Gabriel sat down. "Max said if we stop by tonight, we can read them, or we can come early tomorrow."

"I'll go to the club early tomorrow. I have a full day and don't want to be out too late."

"All right. Tomorrow, after you're done with desk duty, we can sit and chat about any questions we have. Is that good?"

"It works for me." She drank her coffee. Maybe this was a new beginning for both of them.

* * * *

The crowd at Wicked Sanctuary was pretty light for Saturday night. Dani smiled as Allyson and Zeke walked away from the check-in station. Her friend had given her a thumbs up as she walked away.

Gabriel had to cancel Friday at the club. She had been surprised; he'd been excited after dinner Thursday night.

The resignation in his voice told her how unhappy he was about canceling, but his mother arrived unexpectedly, and as much as he'd rather spend time with Dani, he couldn't abandon his mother. She agreed with him; they could talk the following night. His canceling gave her time to think about what he'd put on his questionnaire and what she wanted out of this new relationship with Gabriel.

"I'm surprised there aren't more people here tonight," Dani said to Ralph.

"There's a big concert out at the fairgrounds. I have a feeling a lot of people stayed home instead of trying to deal with the traffic."

"Oh. The club is so far out, and there's rarely traffic on this road. I never thought about it."

"You have to remember our members come from all over; it might be more than traffic on our little road, but the highways can get bogged down."

"True." Dani swallowed. "Ralph, can I ask you a

personal question?"

"Sure, but that doesn't mean I'll answer it."

"Fair enough. Are you into the lifestyle?" Her understanding was that Ralph had been here almost since the opening of Wicked Sanctuary, but she'd never seen him in the club or heard him talk about playing."

"That hasn't been determined yet."

Ralph turned as a couple came inside. As they signed them in, Dani thought about Ralph's answer. He'd been around the lifestyle for years, but wasn't sure if he was part of it.

"Do you want me to stay and keep helping you?" She was a little anxious to get into the club and talk to Allyson.

"Got a hot date with a Dom?" Ralph asked, raising his eyebrows.

"Actually, she does," a male voice said.

Dani looked up to see Gabriel standing there. Her body heated.

"Very good." Ralph signed Gabriel in and looked at her. "Go have fun. I know Gabriel will take care of you."

Dani wondered about Ralph's words but pushed them to the back of her mind as she stood. Gabriel was right there.

"Give me two minutes to put my stuff in a locker, and I'll escort you in."

"I can take care of myself."

"You. Will. Wait."

The way Gabriel said the words practically had her falling to her knees. Damn that Dom voice. She didn't know what else to call it. All the Doms seemed to have it, but only Gabriel affected her that way. "Yes, Sir."

Gabriel nodded and disappeared into the men's room. True to his word, he was back out within minutes. He slipped his arm around her waist and guided her into the club.

The music reminded her of a combination of hip-hop, pop, and dance-at-home music. She started moving her head in time with the music as Gabriel led her across the room to one of the sofa sectionals. He gestured for her to sit, and he sat down beside her, his thigh brushing hers.

That darn heat invaded her body once again as if someone had turned on a space heater right over her head. She wanted to shift away, but she didn't. If she and Gabriel were going to be friends, let alone Dom and sub, she needed to get used to her body's reaction to him.

She kept her voice low and quiet. "Now that we're here..."

"You and I are going to talk. You read my questionnaire as I read yours. And tonight, I'm going to become your Dom. The only one you will ever need."

"Arrogant much, Sir?" She wanted to laugh but couldn't. She'd fantasized the past few days about having Gabriel as her Dom.

"Good thing you tacked on the sir, or I might feel the need to punish you." He stared down at her.

"Can you blame me, Sir. That declaration gave no room for my feelings or my needs."

Gabriel blinked. "You're right. I'm playing the caveman, but you seem to bring out that side of me."

"I think we both have things to work on, Sir. You bring out the brat in me."

He laughed. "I think I can handle a brat once in a while."

Dani bit her lip to prevent herself from grinning. "I bet you can, Sir."

* * * *

Gabriel noticed that Dani was yawning and rubbing her eyes. They'd been talking for a while now. What time was it? He reached for his phone, but it was in his locker, and he didn't wear a watch. "Noah, what time is it?" Noah was chatting with Emily, one of the subs.

"It's after midnight."

"Thanks." No wonder Dani was yawning. She had to be tired. "I think we've talked enough. Are you okay with everything we talked about?"

"Yes, Sir," she said through another yawn. "Dang, I'm sorry."

"It's okay. Come on, I'll walk you to your car." He helped her from the sofa and guided her out of the club to the bathrooms.

While Dani changed, Gabriel got his wallet, keys, and cell phone from his locker. When he came out, he saw Max standing with Dani, chatting.

Dani had pulled on a pair of black pants over her shorts and a T-shirt over that wonderful ruby red bustier she'd worn tonight. Gabriel grinned when he saw the pink sneakers on her feet. "Cute," he said.

"I like to make a fashion statement." She looked up at Max.

"That you do." Max grinned. "Thanks for being available next Sunday."

"Of course, Master Max," Dani said.

"Have a great rest of your weekend." Max walked back into the club.

"What was that about?" Gabriel asked.

"New computer system. Max is having Ralph and me trained next Sunday."

Gabriel walked Dani out to her car and stood there while she unlocked it and got in. She started her vehicle, and rolled down the window.

"Call me when you get home, please."

"Oh." Dani pulled her cell out and punched a button. His phone rang, and she started laughing. "Tarzan yell. Are you kidding me?"

The amusement in her voice made him grin. "That's only for people who are not in my contact list. Once I put you there, you'll get your own ring tone." With his job, it was easier to assign ring tones. Plus, it was kind of fun. "Be careful driving home."

She chuckled and shook her head as she placed her phone on the passenger seat. "Protective Doms. I can call you, but you can't take your phone into the club."

"Humor me." Gabriel stepped away as she put her vehicle into gear and backed out. He kept his gaze on her car until he could no longer see it. Tonight was a new beginning for both of them. And this time, he wouldn't screw it up.

Turning, Gabriel walked back into the club, but he didn't go inside. Instead, he stood by the doors. Lucky for him, Max was in the reception area. "Have a second?"

"What's up? Sierra is waiting for me," Max said.

"This shouldn't take long. I messed up with Dani more than once."

"It looks like things are better now."

That was Max calling it as it was. "I'm pretty sure she's going to agree to give me a chance, and I don't want to mess it up again."

"What do you need from me?"

"Advice. I got advice at the Dom meeting, but I'd like to hear from you."

"No one is perfect, but Dani is more experienced now. You read her questionnaire. Did she tell you about San

Francisco?"

"She did." Did she leave something out of the story? His gut clenched.

"Good. She has more experience than I think you realize."

"She told me she's more of a novice."

Max chuckled. "Why is it some subs either think they're not experienced enough or they're over-experienced. There is no middle ground with them." He shook his head. "Go with your instincts. I don't think you'll scare her this time."

"I hope you're right, because I'm going to be honest with you, Max. If this goes sideways, I don't know what I'm going to do. I enjoy the club, but I don't think I can tolerate seeing Dani play with another Dom."

"I don't believe you need to worry about that. But I'll tell you what I've told all the other Doms. Don't go in making problems. Go in with solutions."

"That makes sense. Thanks for taking time. Enjoy your evening with Sierra." Gabriel turned and walked out to his truck. He sat there, thinking about what Max said until his phone rang; the Tarzan yell made him smile.

"Hey, Dani."

"You assigned me a ring tone that fast?"

The laughter in her voice lightened this heart and his mood. "Not yet. I need to come up with something perfect for you. Are you home?"

"Yes, I am."

"Thank you for calling me. I'll give you a call Monday. I'd like us to have dinner together."

"Sounds good." He could hear her yawn over the phone. "Good night, Gabriel."

"Sweet dreams." Gabriel tossed his phone onto the

passenger seat. He had a lot to think about, but he also had plans to make.

He was going to do things the right way with Dani this time. There would be no reason for her to run from him.

* * * *

Gabriel pulled up in front of Dani's apartment Monday evening. After all the advice he'd gotten at the Dom meeting yesterday, he thought long and hard about where to take her to dinner. He ended up making a reservation at The Aztec Chef.

He'd been lucky and was able to put in a request for one of the private booths in the back of the restaurant. It would give them some privacy. Gabriel stopped at the double door entrance to Dani's building and pressed the button for her apartment.

"Hello." Her voice was tentative, and that surprised him.

"It's Gabriel."

"Oh, hi, Gabriel." Her voice was brighter and stronger now. "I'll be right there."

The line went dead before he could say anything more. Why didn't she buzz him into her apartment? It wasn't like he hadn't been there already. He would talk with her about that over dinner. He paced the small landing area until Dani came bouncing down the hallway and pushed open the door.

He took in the white and yellow sundress she was wearing along with the white sandals on her feet. She could barely stand still, as if she was ready to pounce out of her own skin.

"You didn't tell me where were going; I hope this is okay?"

"It's just fine. We're going for Mexican." He cupped

her elbow and guided her toward his vehicle. "Thank you for allowing me to drive you." They'd had a disagreement about who should drive, but he'd pulled her around to his way of thinking.

"So how was your day today?" he asked as he pulled out onto the main road.

"It was fine. I had a nice long conversation with Max and Sierra about the plants they want around their home."

"I know you're doing the landscaping for the club, but you're also doing it for their home?" Why did that surprise him? Dani was the best in the business.

"Yep. The house and the club are big jobs, but I'm up to it, and I have good crews to help me."

"You took everything over from your grandfather, right?"

"Yes." She shifted in her seat. "After his heart attack, we had a long talk. He agreed he needed to slow down, so I took over. I will say the crews were very grateful. Many of them were worried the business would close, and they would lose their jobs."

"I can understand that. I will also say I was surprised to see you came home to stay." He figured she was in San Francisco for good. What could Pleasant Valley offer her that San Francisco didn't have?

"I always planned to come back. When I was offered the job right before we graduated, I decided to take it. It was a large landscaping operation, and it gave me the experience and knowledge I needed. Though I didn't really like being a cog in the wheel." She glanced at him and out the window. "Besides, Pleasant Valley is my home."

Gabriel smiled. "It's my home, too, and I can't see leaving it. I'm glad you're home." Even though he hadn't expected to see her at the bookstore that day, he'd had a sneaking suspicion she'd moved back home.

"I'm really glad to be home. I'd forgotten just how much it means to be part of a community."

Gabriel pondered her words as he pulled into the parking lot of the restaurant. He took Dani's hand as they walked inside. She gave him a pointed look but didn't pull away. Score one for the home team.

The festive music and colorful decorations made him smile. He gave his name to the hostess, and they were immediately shown to their booth. Dani gave him a sharp look when she saw the booth in the back of the restaurant.

He released her hand, and she slid onto the seat. He followed, not stopping until his thigh touched hers. The hostess set the menus on the table and walked away.

"I think I understand why you chose here," Dani said, inching away.

Gabriel picked up the menus and handed her one. "I knew they had these booths, and here, we are less likely to be overheard."

She nodded and opened her menu. Gabriel took a brief glance at his. He hadn't been to The Aztec Chef in a while. He looked up as the waiter stopped in front of their table.

"Good evening. I'm Juan, your waiter for the evening. May I get you a margarita or something else to drink?"

"A pineapple margarita would be lovely," Dani said.

"I'd love a beer. Whatever you have on tap that is dark."

"Very good, sir."

"And a glass of water, please," Dani tacked on.

"Of course. Tonight, we offer the triple plate special, and the vegetarian special is a spinach bean salad. I'll go get your drinks and be back for your order."

Dani looked from Gabriel to the menu he'd set aside

and back. "You've already decided on what you want to eat, haven't you?"

"Yes. I know what I like."

"What do you recommend?"

Gabriel's eyebrows rose. "You're asking my opinion?" This was different. Even when they were in college, she rarely asked for his recommendation.

"I told you some things have changed, and I haven't been here for years."

That was true. They'd both changed. At least, he hoped he had. "The enchiladas are good, as are the burritos. I'd keep away from the special as it's a lot of food. Pretty much everything is good."

"Thank you." She closed her menu and set it down. "So how much alcohol do I need to get through our dinner?"

Gabriel almost burst out laughing. "That's an interesting question. I will only have one beer, and I suspect you probably won't need more than the margarita." He kept his gaze on her.

"How are we..." She broke off as the waiter approached the table.

Juan set down her margarita, water, and Gabriel's beer. "Are you ready to order?" Gabriel looked at her and she nodded.

Dani gave her order, and Gabriel gave his, then turned his attention back to Dani as the waiter walked away.

"We talked Saturday night, but I forgot to ask you a question about your hard limits," Gabriel said.

"Okay."

"You have a hard limit on impression toys. Why?"

"I like spankings." She paused, her cheeks turning pink. "It wasn't as bad as I thought. Light flogging and even use of a paddle. For me, it's a nice way to warm up, feel all tingly, and relax." She looked away, and he patiently waited. When she shivered, Gabriel took up the reins once again.

"That doesn't answer my question." He wanted to know why impression toys bothered her so much. He'd used them a few times on subs who'd requested them, but he was careful.

Her gaze returned to his face, before she lowered her gaze to the table. "It's a little hard to answer."

"Just tell me what you're thinking." Was this why she had run in college? He was the one who brought up spanking and using a paddle. When she freaked out over it, he didn't understand why. Maybe now he would find out the answer.

"When I was in San Francisco at one of the kink parties, there was a demonstration. Unfortunately, that night, my Dom wasn't with me, or he would've steered me away from the demo." Dani closed her eyes.

Gabriel placed his hand over hers. "What kind of demonstration?" Something scared her that night; he could hear it in her voice and see it on her face.

She opened her eyes. "Impact play. At first, I thought it was just normal, but the Dom started using impression paddles, slappers that left impressions, and whips." Dani shivered. "It was horrible."

"Horrible how?"

Dani turned her hand over in his and squeezed his fingers. "He left welts."

"I see. And the sub didn't say her safeword?"

Dani shook her head. "Plus, there was an incident when we were in college."

Gabriel tightened his fingers around hers. "Tell me about it?"

"One of the girls I hung out with, the group of us noticed she had trouble sitting. When we asked her about it, she showed us the bruises her boyfriend left on her ass."

"I see. Why didn't you say anything?" That's why she panicked? Not that he blamed her.

"I wasn't thinking straight that night. And what I saw in the club reinforced my fear."

"I can't guess about your friend in college, but with the party, I suspect the Dom was a sadist and the sub a masochist." He squeezed her hand. "Paddles and slappers from me are instruments of pleasure. There might be a little pain involved, but it morphs into pleasure. I don't cause bruises or break the skin. Any impression slapper I use would only leave an imprint for a few minutes then fade." He drew in a breath. "And I would never use a whip on anyone that wasn't experienced enough to handle it or wanted it ."

"Don't they fall all together?"

"No, they don't." He released her hand and sat back.

"But you make the rules."

"Dani, have you ever used your safe word?"

"Only on you in the club.".

"Have you ever wanted to say it other than to me?"

Her nod was so slight, so fragile, he almost missed it.

"I know you went through the classes at the club. If a sub says her safe word, all play stops."

"But what if the Dom doesn't stop?" Her voice was so quiet he had to strain to hear her.

Gabriel stared at her. "Then he is stopped. We all agree to consent; if a sub says their safe word, they are revoking her consent."

He hadn't picked up this—fear, was the only word he could think of—from her Saturday. What else was Dani hiding? "I'm not sure how they did things in San Francisco, or what your Dom taught you, but I suspect a lot of what you saw may have been about the Master/slave relationship or the 24/7 type of lifestyle. I'm not into those. I'm just talking about the D/s relationship. Dom and sub."

Dani looked a little confused. "So basically what I've been doing in the club?"

"Yes and no." Gabriel broke off as the waiter arrived with tortilla chips and salsa. "Since I haven't seen you play at the club, I don't know what you've done. So I'm assuming that it's a typical type of light play."

"Mainly just a little bondage and some sensation play."

"Good. What I'm talking about is what we would do inside and outside the club. We would only play with each other unless there was something you wanted to try that I was not comfortable doing."

Her mouth dropped open. "You'd let me play with another Dom?"

"I'd rather not. But if there is something you really want to try, we would talk about it. If it's something I know in my heart I couldn't give you and you really wanted to try, I would allow you to try it with someone else. Someone I trusted."

"What about you? What if there's something you want to try, and I can't do it?"

"We would talk about it and make a decision at that point. The odds of me playing with another sub are minimal. I do need to let you know that sometimes Doms will come to me for instruction on impact play and offer up their sub for me to use."

Dani stared at him. "So you teach other Doms?"

"Yes. Max believes in mentoring the younger Doms. We've set it up so they're able to come to us and ask us for instruction or questions, especially when it's something new to them. Most are very open about it, but if someone wants a private lesson, I will come to you and tell you. I will also make it clear that I want you in the room."

"What if the Dom asks you to do something, let's say, with the whip?"

Gabriel shook his head. "I rarely work with whips anymore, so I would only do it if Max asked me to. I'm not a Dom who likes to leave marks on a sub's body. That hasn't changed. There are sadists in the club, and that's fine. Their kink is not my kink. Does that help?"

"It does. I didn't realize how much I still don't know about the lifestyle."

"There are a lot of aspects to the lifestyle, and I don't think we truly learn them all. We learn what we like and what we dislike. Communication and consent are the two most important things."

"I think that's what drew me to Wicked Sanctuary. Some of the clubs in San Francisco weren't as consensual as I think they should have been. I avoided them and parties like that. I also need to clarify that, while I may be a club member, I haven't played very much."

"Why is that?" Surprise flooded him. He had expected she'd played every week since she was already at the club.

"I was getting a feel for the club. I've only played with one or two of the Doms, and they've all been nice."

"They'd better have been. But they're done playing with you. You're mine."

Dani frowned, and he realized just how much like a Dom he sounded. "I haven't played in a while either. Actually, it's been several months."

"Why is that?" Her hand froze as she lifted a chip to her mouth. "I shouldn't have asked that." She lowered her hand.

"At the time, I wasn't finding any satisfaction in playing at the club." Gabriel cupped her chin and turned her face to him. "There is nothing you can't ask me. I mean that, absolutely nothing. I do reserve the right to say I'm not going to answer, but feel free to ask me. That goes for both of us. I meant it when I said communication is important. If we don't talk to each other, I don't know what's going on in your head. Contrary to popular belief, Doms are not mind readers."

She laughed. "If you guys could read minds, we'd all be in trouble."

Wasn't that the truth. The subs in the club weren't normally a bratty bunch. They were pretty well behaved. But he'd seen some subs who wanted to be disciplined, so they acted like a brat on purpose. Nothing wrong with that, just not his thing, and he suspected not Dani's.

"So how are we going to do this?"

"How do you think we should do it?" Gabriel picked up a chip, dipped it in the salsa, and ate it while Dani pondered his question.

"We do have a history together." She took a sip of her margarita. "But I feel strongly that we need to get to know each other again."

Gabriel chewed and swallowed. "Yes, we do."

"So that means more dates?"

Her voice was soft and her tone tentative. Gabriel ate another chip while thinking over her question. More dates? For sure. He wanted a relationship with Dani, not just club play. He finished his chip and stared at her. "Yes, more dates."

"What about at the club?"

"What would you like to do?"

Dani huffed. "Would you quit throwing my questions back at me? You're supposed to be the Dom."

"I'm a Dom, not a dictator. I want your input. This is a two-way street. In the club, I'm your Dom, in the bedroom, I'm your Dom. Outside of that, I'm your friend and moving my way back to being your boyfriend, I hope."

Dani stared at him, and he could almost see the wheels turning behind her eyes. She hadn't expected him to say that.

"That's a lot to think about, especially the boyfriend part."

"Which is why we're having dinner tonight. I know the way we parted in college was not the best, but I'd like us to start over."

Chapter 5

Dani was stunned. Gabriel wanted to be her boyfriend again? She hadn't expected that. He'd made it clear he wanted to be her Dom in and out of the club.

Playing with Gabriel inside the club? Yes. She wanted that. It had taken her some time to come to those terms, but her body thrummed for Gabriel, and she wanted to explore kink with him. But outside of it? Dani's emotions were all over the place. Their breakup a couple of months before graduation, while traumatic, was expected. At least, she'd figured it would happen.

Had he changed? Dani almost laughed. Not in just a few weeks. No one could change that fast, though she recognized the irony. She'd been the one telling him things had changed and now, when he told her something that had changed, she…

It was hard for her to put her faith in him.

Her trust in him had been broken, but on some level, she'd begun trusting him again; otherwise, she would have shut him down at the club and wouldn't even consider dating him.

"I need to think about this more."

He frowned. "I thought this was what you wanted."

"Tonight, I'm not so sure." She put her hands on the table. It wasn't like her to be so indecisive. "We've been apart for a few years. I'm willing to try some club play, but a relationship… I'm just not sure about that yet." Would she ever be sure of it? *Yes*, her heart yelled. *Take the plunge.*

Gabriel's warm hand covered hers on the table. "I'm sorry I hurt you in college. I know I handled kink wrong. I also know my reactions to you in the past few weeks weren't the best. All I can do now is to show you I'm worthy of your trust. If you'll give me the chance."

The waiter returned with their meals, and Gabriel let go of her hand. She missed his warmth. The food was set down in front of them, and the waiter left.

"Let's enjoy dinner and get to know each other again," Gabriel said.

Dani nodded and glanced down at her plate. The food looked delicious, but she could only stare at it. Was there too much past between them? And what about the secret she was keeping from him? She picked at her meal and noticed Gabriel doing much of the same.

"I put a damper on our evening; I'm sorry," she said.

"You gave us both a lot to think about, and that's not a bad thing." Gabriel signaled the waiter.

"Is there something wrong with the food, sir?"

"Everything is fine. We're just not as hungry as we thought. If you could box up the food to go, I would really appreciate it."

"Of course, sir." The waiter swept up the plates and walked away.

"I really am sorry, Gabriel."

"There's nothing to be sorry about. You're right to be cautious, and I get it. We both have a lot of thinking to do, and I suggest we take a few days to do that. Does that work for you?"

"Yes, it does." He was willing to give her time. Now, if she could just straighten out her own head.

* * * *

Dani walked around the pool area of Max and Sierra's home Friday morning while she waited for Sierra to come outside. Sierra had called her yesterday and asked that she come out. Dani agreed, but wondered what was going on. She and Sierra had already agreed on the landscaping plan for the front of the house. The back area was already beautifully done with lots of plants and trees, so she wasn't exactly sure what Sierra wanted her to do.

She turned around when the patio door opened. The last person she expected to see walk out was Gabriel. They hadn't talked since Monday night. That hadn't stopped him from texting her. On one hand, his attention flattered her. But she was still trying to wrap her head around their dinner.

Damn, he looked good in those jeans, work boots, and that chest-hugging, long-sleeve shirt. Her heart jumped. He'd filled out since college, and she had to say he looked damn sexy. His dark hair was mussed, as if he'd been running his fingers through it.

"Dani, I didn't realize you were here," he said.

"I'm just waiting for Sierra. She wanted to talk about the plans out here."

"Max sent me out here to wait for him so we could talk about remodeling."

Dani tilted her head and stared at Gabriel. "Do you think those two are matchmaking?"

Gabriel gave a husky laugh. "I wouldn't put anything past them." He walked down the stairs toward Dani. "How are you doing?"

"Fine. Work is busy, which is good."

"That's not what I meant." Gabriel cupped her cheek. "We haven't had time to talk. I want to know if you're okay after our discussion Monday night."

"I could ask you the same thing." Why was she tempted to sink into his embrace and just lay her head against his chest? It'd been like that in college. Whenever Dani had a bad day or was trying to work out a problem, Gabriel would just hold her and let her be in the moment, to think.

"You could. But for me, nothing is changed. I want to be with you."

Her heart pounded, and her body heated. If she was honest with herself, she wanted that too. But a tiny bit of fear simmered in the back of her mind. "Can we try in the club first and go from there?" That was a good compromise.

"If that's how you want to start, I'm agreeable."

Relief flowed through Dani's veins. "I'm being cautious; I know."

Gabriel shifted, bringing his body closer to hers. "You do what's best for you. I'm not going anywhere."

She opened her mouth to reply when the patio doors opened again, and Max and Sierra walked out. She took a step back from Gabriel, and his hand fell from her cheek.

Max took Sierra's hand as they walked down the stairs. "I'm glad we've got you both here," Max said. "We want to expand the patio area and the back area of the club to create some special gardens."

Dani glanced around and looked back at Max. "What kind of special gardens?" Dani asked.

"The kind that will allow people to have some, shall we say, sexy outdoor fun." Max grinned.

"Really, Max," Sierra said, playfully hitting him on the shoulder.

"Now that sounds very interesting." Gabriel threw Dani a sexy grin.

"That's why we wanted both of you here," Sierra said. "To discuss the ideas and see what is possible."

"Let's sit down and talk about this." Max led Sierra her over to the patio tables and pulled out a chair for her. Dani followed, not surprised when Gabriel held a chair out for her.

"Thank you," she whispered.

Gabriel didn't say anything, but his hands brushed over her shoulders before he sat down next to her.

For the next hour, Max outlined what he wanted to do to the pool area and outside the club as well.

"I can check out where the electrical and plumbing runs. We might have to run some new lines. Plus, I would have to work with Dani closely; there are a lot of trees in the areas you're talking about."

"That's true." Dani had been making little sketches on her tablet. "I'll need to check local ordinances since this is adding to what we're already doing. I know it's not a building, but we'd be removing a lot of trees."

"We'll replace them," Sierra said.

"I know you will, but I have to check the regulations. Even though this is private land, the state and city can be very picky about how much forest is impacted." She made a note on her tablet. "Gabriel and I will have to get together and figure out a schedule once everything is laid out." Working with Gabriel would be interesting.

"I can do the sketching and so forth, but I'll need Zeke's crew to do the work. How soon do you want a proposal?" Gabriel asked.

"I would think you would want to have the work completed before winter sets in," Dani said.

"That would be ideal," Max said. "But we're not on a tight timeframe or anything."

Gabriel sat back in his chair. "All right, let's start with getting some plans together and seeing what kind of permits, if any, we need, and we can go from there." He turned toward Dani. "Does that work for you?"

"Yes. Remember, if we need permits, they could take a week to several months."

"That's why our timeline is rather flexible," Max said. "Plus, I know Zeke will do the work, and he is overloaded with jobs right now."

"He is. That's why I'm helping him supervise the construction guys out here at the club," Gabriel said. "I'll check with Zeke and see who's available, and I'll take care of them."

"I'll start researching the forest ordinances and some possible plans that'll work with what you want to do." Dani made more notes on her tablet.

"Anything else?" Max asked.

"I don't—" Dani's phone rang. "Excuse me for a moment." She stood and pulled her phone out of her back pocket, taking a few steps away before answering. "This is Dani."

"It's Jeff. Did those new succulents come in for the Mason job?"

"They should've come in first thing this morning."

"That's what I thought. I just talked with Lydia, and she said there were no deliveries so far today."

Dani rubbed her forehead. Great, another late delivery. "Have Lydia call them and tell them they must be delivered today. You have enough to do on the Mason job. Putting in the succulents can wait till tomorrow, but we have to have those plants."

"You got it, boss. I just wanted to make sure no one had called you."

The line went dead, and Dani rubbed her forehead with her free hand as she put her phone away. Late deliveries were getting to be a habit lately. She might have to find a new supplier.

"Problem?" Gabriel asked as he walked up to her. Dani glanced up and noticed that Max and Sierra were gone.

"Just a late delivery. Where did Max and Sierra go?"

"They didn't have anything else to tell us. And Sierra needed to go to her office."

"That makes sense. I sometimes forget that Sierra still has a job." She walked back over to the table and picked up her tablet. "I need to get moving. I have a couple of the jobs I need to check in on."

"I'll walk out with you," Gabriel said.

Instead of walking back to the house, Gabriel guided her around the side and out the small gate to where their vehicles were parked.

"Your car wasn't here when I arrived," she said.

"No. I drove over from the club since I knew once this talk was done, I would be off to my next commitment." He stood with her next to her vehicle. "Are you coming to the club tonight?"

"I have to work the door first, but then I'll be in."

"I'll be there as well. Can we walk around the club together?"

Dani pondered his question for half second. "I'd like that." She didn't miss the gleam of excitement that flashed in Gabriel's eyes.

"Great. Have a good rest of your day." Gabriel leaned over and brushed a kiss over her cheek.

Dani froze. The feel of Gabriel's kiss on her cheek sent a shockwave of sensation through her body. It wasn't as if he hadn't kissed her before, but this felt different. This felt new.

"I'll see you later." Her voice was soft. She opened the door to her vehicle, climbed in, and drove away. Between this job, playing at the club, and possibly dating, she and Gabriel were definitely going to be seeing more of each other. That send a shaft of excitement and anticipation through her body.

* * * *

Gabriel strode into Wicked Sanctuary. He was later than he wanted to be, but he'd done that on purpose. He wanted to sign in without Dani being at the check-in desk. After changing his clothes, he walked into the club.

He stopped inside the door and closed his eyes. The techno beat of the music soaked into his skin, and he relaxed. He wanted to be here. He needed to be here. He opened his eyes and scanned the club for Dani.

There she was, waiting in the green area and talking with some of the other subs. He started to move in that direction but stopped when another Dom approach Dani. Gabriel's hackles rose. Dani was his.

Down, boy. They'd only agreed to walking around the club tonight. He crossed the room and was stopped by Max.

"You have that look in your eyes," Max said.

Gabriel took a deep breath. "I won't do anything without her full agreement. We've talked and come to an understanding."

"Very well." Max stepped out of his way, and Gabriel continued his journey. First chance he got, he'd convince Dani to change the wristband she wore to purple and white to signify taken sub. Gabriel didn't recognize the Dom who was talking to Dani, but he didn't know everyone in the club. Dani glanced up as he approached, her brown eyes sparkling.

"Good evening, Dani." Gabriel nodded at the other Dom. "Are you ready to walk around the club with me?" He held out his hand.

"Yes, Sir. I am." She put her hand in his, and his confidence soared. "Sorry, Sir," she said to the other Dom. "As I was explaining, I've promised my time to Sir Gabriel tonight."

"Very well," the Dom said, but his gaze never left Dani. "Maybe another night. I'll be keeping my eyes on you." The man walked away.

A shiver went through Dani's body. "Are you okay?" Gabriel watched the Dom head for the other side of the club. He would keep his eyes on the man. Something didn't feel right.

"Let's walk around," she said. "See you ladies later."

Gabriel smiled at the subs, put his arm around Dani's waist, and guided her away. "Was the Dom saying things to you that you didn't like?"

"He's just one of the newer ones. I've seen him play with the couple the subs, and I don't like his attitude."

"Oh?" Gabriel would definitely keep his eye on the man and tell Max. Even with all the screenings Max did, sometimes a bad apple slipped through.

"Thank you for coming to my rescue. I do appreciate it."

"It really wasn't a rescue. I know you can take care of yourself, and I'm sure if you told him no, he would've walked away." As any Dom in the club should when a sub said no.

"Maybe."

Gabriel frowned and pulled Dani to a stop. Her tone was too skeptical, and he didn't like it. "If you have any doubts about this Dom, you should talk to Max."

Dani shook her head. "It's probably nothing. Just me."

"I don't think so." Gabriel spied Max by the bar, talking with Zeke. He guided Dani in that direction, and she stiffened in his hold. But he wasn't going to let this go. Couldn't let this go. Max wouldn't want him to, and Dani's instincts were good ones. He knew that from college where he'd witnessed her calling out some of the guys on campus for hassling women. "Max, do you have a minute?"

"Of course. Is there an issue between you two?" Max's gaze roamed over the possessive hold Gabriel had on Dani.

"No," Gabriel said. He looked down at Dani, and she shifted from one foot to the other.

"Dani, do you need to speak to me alone?" Max asked.

"No, Master Max. It's just…" She hesitated, but Gabriel wanted her to tell the story. She chewed her lip for a moment, then spoke up. "It's the new Dom. Ward is his name."

Max frowned, and Dani cuddled closer to Gabriel. Was she worried Max would be angry with her?

"You seem hesitant," Max said. "May I?" Max held up his hand and looked at Gabriel.

Gabriel nodded.

Max took Dani's hand in his. "You know you can tell me anything. Anything at all."

"Yes, Master Max. All of us know we can come to you about anything when something is bothering us."

"Good to know. So can you explain your hesitation?"

Gabriel tightened his arm around her waist to let her know he was there for her and to lend her strength.

"The problem is, I don't have anything concrete. It's just a feeling. When he talks to me, his choice of words and his tone make my skin crawl. And…" Dani took a deep breath. "Some of the other subs indicated he doesn't like to take no for an answer."

"I see." Max released her hand, glanced over at Zeke, and nodded. He turned his attention back to Dani. "Ward needs several refresher classes. Thank you for bringing this to my attention. Please remind the subs that if a Dom doesn't listen to their no, even on the first time, I want to know. I will not tolerate a Dom disrespecting a sub in my club."

Dani sagged against Gabriel. She'd been really wound up about this, and he wondered why. Maybe it had something to do with her time in San Francisco. She'd mentioned that some of the places she went to worried her that consent was ignored.

"Thank you, Max," Gabriel said. "Dani and I are going to walk around the club, but I appreciate your attention to this matter."

"Of course. I want the subs in my club to feel comfortable and not have to worry that their concerns will not be heard." Max looked at Gabriel and tilted his head.

Gabriel nodded.

Max leaned down and kissed Dani on the forehead. "You're one of the family. I will make sure you are taken care of, and I'm sure Gabriel will as well."

Dani's cheeks turned pink, and Gabriel grinned as he guided Dani away from Max and toward a flogging scene. "Are you okay now?"

"Yes, Sir." Dani blew out a breath. "It's always a little nerve-racking to talk with Master Max, especially in the club."

Gabriel turned Dani to face him. "Why?"

"He seems…so powerful, so in control that it's almost scary."

Gabriel's grinned. "You didn't seem to feel that way

when you were talking to him about the landscaping."

"Outside the club, he's different. It's hard to explain. An aura of power is around him, but inside the club, it's almost tangible."

Gabriel stared down at her as he pondered her words. He never viewed Max any differently in or out of the club, but he was beginning to think maybe the subs did. "Do you view me differently?"

"Not really. But we haven't played together yet."

"You played with Max?" A shockwave went through his body.

"Not the way you're thinking. Max guided me a bit in training one night when Bennett wasn't available, of course this was before he met Sierra."

Relief filled Gabriel. "I understand now. I was thinking we could watch this flogging scene and discuss it. Does that work for you?"

Her eyes brightened. "Yes, Sir, it does."

Gabriel led Dani over to the scene and found a spot for them to watch. His attention wasn't on the scene; it was on Dani. She was a very strong woman. He'd noticed that outside the club. She had to be since she ran her own business. But inside the club, she was so very different. Were all subs like that?

He hadn't really been around the other subs outside the club, except maybe Allyson. Well, there was Lara, but they never interacted that much. Dani was teaching him things he'd never thought about. It wasn't a bad thing; it just made him aware that he had more to learn.

When the scene ended, he led Dani to one of the quiet areas, and they sat down. "What did you think of the scene?"

"It was very sensual."

Gabriel had known it would be; it was why he picked that one and the couple. "How did you feel about Zeke flogging Allyson?"

"It was like they were each playing a role. I really like how Zeke stopped and checked in with Allyson often."

"A good Dom should always check in with the sub as the playing progresses. Have you not observed that?"

"I didn't mean it that way. I've seen the way the Doms here treat their subs. How much attention they pay to them and make sure they're okay. In San Francisco, at some of the parties, the Doms didn't do that."

"I see." He had some work to do to show her that he was more like the Doms here than anywhere else. "Is there anything you'd like to try tonight?" He kept his gaze on her face, but Dani was silent. He'd wait. She had to make the decision not him.

"I'd like to try something very simple and basic, Sir."

"I'm open to anything you want to do. What do you have in mind?" They were starting out new together, and regardless of having been past lovers, they needed to learn each other's bodies all over again.

"The massage table, Sir."

"Good choice." Gabriel glanced over her shoulder. The massage area was empty. "Let me go check to make sure no one is signed up for the area, and I'll be right back." Gabriel stood and walked across the room. After checking the sign-up sheet, he climbed on the stage and wiped down the equipment.

He knew the requirement was that the equipment be wiped down after each use, but he always made sure everything was clean. He wouldn't take any chances. Gabriel looked over toward Dani, who was watching him. He put a sheet on the table and motioned her over. Gabriel kept his gaze on her. His cock pulsed with every step she took toward him.

He wasn't surprised by his body's reaction. Dani had done that to him even in college. When she stopped in front of the stage, he held out his hand and helped her up the stairs. "Do you want a full body massage or just your back?"

"I'm open to whatever you want to do, Sir."

Gabriel pondered her words. "Are you okay with me touching you intimately?" There was only so much he could do in the beginning, but at least this would get her used to his touch.

"Yes, Sir. It's fine."

"All right. I'll let you get undressed, and I'll get some oil and towels. Please wait until I return, so I can help you onto the table." Gabriel didn't wait to see if she obeyed his orders. He went over to the storage closet by the bar, grabbed some vanilla rose oil, and took several towels from the stack.

Dani was standing next to the table. Nude. His breath left his body. Gorgeous. Sexy. His. These were the words that came to him. Her back was straight, her breasts thrust out, and her gaze on him. Pride swelled in him. His woman wasn't afraid of anything. He set the oil and towels on the side table and approached Dani. He put his hands on her waist.

"You know I could do this by myself, Sir." She placed her hands on his shoulders.

"Of course you can." He lifted her onto the table. "But what's the fun in that? I like touching you."

Her cheeks filled with color. "Face up or face down, Sir?"

"Face down, for now." He stayed close as she stretched

out on the table. Once she was comfortable, he reached over and picked up the bottle of oil. He poured some into his palm and set the bottle back down.

Gabriel rubbed his hands together before he placed them on her lower back. She stiffened for just a second and then relaxed. He started massaging her lower back, keeping his palms on her spine as he progressed up to her head.

With each pass up and down her spine and over her back, he could feel her muscles going lax. He concentrated on her shoulders and neck for a few minutes before skimming his fingers over her spine and over her ass to the top of her thighs.

He started with her left leg, massaging it all the way to her toes and moving to her right leg to do the exact same thing. When he finished, he massaged her ass gently. He loved her firm globes. Probably from all the squatting and kneeling she did in her job.

Dani released soft breath when he lifted his hands. He grabbed one of the towels and wiped off his hands. "Time to turn over, love."

He grabbed the pillow to protect Dani's head and helped her turn over. Her skin was slightly flushed; her nipples stood at attention, and her breathing was slow and steady. "Comfortable?" He was very careful when he placed the pillow so he didn't pull her hair.

"Any more comfortable, Sir, and I'd fall asleep."

A chuckle left his lips. "I can't have that." He reached down and tweaked one of her nipples. Dani's eyes went wide, and her mouth opened.

"I'm awake now, Sir." Her voice was breathless.

"Good. Now, I'll start on your front side." Gabriel picked up the bottle of oil and poured some into his palm. It was then he happened to glance up and notice the crowd they'd drawn. He wondered if Dani realized it.

He didn't mind the crowd. But he didn't want Dani to be uncomfortable.

* * * *

Dani drew in a deep breath as Gabriel began to massage her collarbone and above her breasts. The man had magic hands. Her muscles had been tight for most of the night, not because of Gabriel but because of other things. Especially when she told Max about the new Dom.

She wasn't one to complain, but she was a little worried based on what some of the other subs had said. She tried to get them to go to Max, but they kept brushing off their concerns. Gabriel was right to have her talk to Max.

Gabriel running his nails lightly over her nipples brought her attention zinging back to him, where it should've been. Her skin remembered his touch. As he kneaded the knots out of her muscles, she turned to mush.

He tweaked her nipple again, and she almost came off the table. A rush of heat fluttered her pussy, and she wanted more. He ran his hands over her breasts and continued his downward journey over her stomach to her legs.

She fought not to wiggle when he got to her feet and massaged them thoroughly. She wanted more, oh so much more. And she wasn't thinking about the massage. She wanted those hands of his on her breasts and her pussy.

This was the man she remembered. The college lover who was ever so patient and ever so loving. Had they really changed that much since college? She whimpered when Gabriel's touch disappeared.

"How are you doing?" he asked.

"Like I could lay here forever." He'd done such a good job, she wasn't even sure she could move.

His husky chuckle reached her ears. "I'm going to grab

another towel and wipe up the excess oil on your body. This way you can get dressed when you're ready."

"Sir?" Her heart pounded, but she wanted more. Much more.

"Yes, love."

Dani had never been good at asking for what she wanted, but this was Gabriel. This was a man her body knew. "Would you please play with my body, Sir."

His silence made her nervous. Maybe she shouldn't have asked.

"What did you have in mind?"

"Whatever you would like, Sir." She was speaking from her heart now. She was going to jump into this relationship and pray she didn't end up with another broken heart.

"Oh, sweetheart. The trust you have in me." His voice was soft. "Open your eyes, please."

Dani did as requested and saw Gabriel staring down at her. In his gaze, she saw need and acceptance. "I do trust you." That was never a question in her mind. Gabriel would never hurt her. "I always did."

Gabriel looked stunned. "Let's get you cleaned up and off the table. I can clean up the scene; you can dress, and we'll decide what we want to do next."

"Yes, Sir." A thrill of excitement ran through her veins. It was time to explore with Gabriel. Past time. She wasn't going to mess it up this time.

Chapter 6

Gabriel cleaned up the area and equipment, but his mind was in turmoil. A good turmoil. Dani wanted to play tonight. He hadn't expected that. The massage was to show her he could take things slow with her. But it had turned into so much more.

The feel of her silky skin beneath his fingers. The tiny shivers that coursed through her body as he touched her. And those breathy little sighs. He hadn't realized how much he'd missed them.

He kept an eye on Dani as she dressed. She seemed steady, and it wasn't like they'd played. But still, she'd been so relaxed. He finished cleaning up and returned the bottle of oil. Noah was at the bar, so he asked him for two bottles of water and walked back to Dani.

He guided her off the stage and over to the aftercare area. He waited for her to say anything, but Dani stayed silent. Gabriel put his arm around her waist, sat down, and pulled her into his lap. He set one water bottle on the sofa and opened the other one.

"Drink up," he said, handing her the bottle.

Dani accepted the bottle from him and took a long healthy drink. "Thank you, Sir. I hadn't realized how thirsty I was." She rested her head on his shoulder.

"I like you in my arms." While Dani had muscle on her, she still felt very delicate to him. "How are you feeling? Still like a wet noodle?"

"I'm doing better, Sir."

"Drop the sir for right now. What else did you have in mind for tonight?"

She scrunched up her nose, and he wanted to kiss the wrinkles away. She was so cute when she was thinking.

"I don't know, except that I want your hands on my body."

"Hmmm, I'm not sure what kind of scene we can have." Gabriel sat quietly for a few minutes. "If that's all you want for tonight, and I know it's a little early for this, but what do you say about taking this private."

"Private?"

"Yes. My place or yours. For me, the club isn't the place for intimate touching, not unless we're doing a full-blown scene." He waited, but Dani stayed silent. "If you'd rather stay here, I understand. We can cuddle on the couch."

Dani shook her head. "It's not that. I'm trying to understand." She bit her lower lip. "I didn't see you as the type to hesitate to play in public."

"You said you wanted my hands on your body, and I don't feel right doing that for the first time in the club where people can see us. I want to relearn what you like and don't like, but I'd rather do that in private. Besides, here in the club, we can't have sex."

"And who says were going to have sex?"

A smile curved his lips at the outrage in her voice, but it also had a twinge of laughter.

"Let me correct that: if we have sex. There is no pressure. We will just let our bodies do the talking for us. Is that acceptable?"

"It is. Shall we go to your place? I can follow you in my car." Gabriel frowned as Dani held up her hand. "Before you start to argue, that would be the easiest way—that way I can drive myself home without us having to come back for my car."

"Always practical."

She was right. He dropped a kiss on her nose.

"Let's sit here for a few more minutes and then we'll go."

"All right." She wiggled and settled more comfortably against him. Gabriel willed his dick to behave. In a short time, Dani would be at his place and in his bed. The night couldn't end better.

* * * *

"This is a nice neighborhood," Dani said as she exited her car. She thought he lived in an apartment, but he drove into one of the newly developed areas of Pleasant Valley. "Did you design these homes?"

"Yes." He put his arm around her waist, and her heart did a pitter-patter in her chest. "Zeke did the construction, and I reserved one of the homes."

She wasn't surprised. She liked the way the homes were set apart from each other. "Outside of designing them, how involved in the construction were you?" Even though it was dark, he had outdoor lighting that showed the beautiful landscaping of the homes. "I did the landscaping, or at least, I should say the company did." She recognized those plants. Golden Euonymus bushes. They had been specifically asked for when she did these houses.

Gabriel chuckled. "You did. Zeke likes hiring local companies. As for my involvement, it was mainly drawing up the plans and making adjustments. One thing we did for this development was different. We agreed to as much customization as possible without having to go back to the permit office."

"Does that happen a lot?" It was one of the reasons she went to an apartment rather than a home. She was going to need something customized for her and maybe her business.

"Going back to the permit office? Sometimes. As for the customization, some builders don't like to do that; it can be a nightmare. But Zeke has found that when he offers the customization, the houses sell faster, and people are happier."

"That makes sense." He guided her up the two steps to the front porch and opened the front door.

"Welcome to my home." Gabriel gestured for her to enter.

Dani stepped inside, and the hall light came on. "Automatic lights?" The lights gleamed off the dark hardwood floor. She loved hardwood.

"Motion detected." He led her down the hallway and into the family room.

The forest green sofa looked warm and inviting with a familiar looking crocheted quilt draped over the back. It was perpendicular to a matching recliner she could picture Gabriel sitting in to watch the football game on his big screen TV. "I see Grandma is keeping up with her crochet skills."

"That she is. She wouldn't listen to me when I wanted her to keep it and give it to you." He drew her into his arms. "Have you changed your mind about spending the night with me?"

"I have not, but we both need to be open about how we feel if this relationship is going to progress."

"Agreed." He lowered his head and captured her lips with his.

Dani sighed into his mouth. She wrapped her arms around his neck and sank her fingers into his hair. He cradled her to his body. His touch and kiss were achingly familiar. His hands roamed up and down her back, creating delicious sensations that flowed through her body.

Skin. She wanted her body against his with nothing between them. She broke the kiss long enough to whip his T-shirt over his head before their lips met in another long, hard kiss. She couldn't get enough of him. This was the Gabriel she remembered. The considerate lover. The lover who made her feel feminine yet powerful.

Dani slid her fingers over his chest, and her palms flattened against the rough hair. His heart was racing. She was sure hers was as well. She enjoyed the feeling of his coarse hair against her skin. But there was more. There was muscle that hadn't been there before.

He broke the kiss, his lips trailing from her mouth to her ear. He gently bit the lobe. She shivered in anticipation of what he would do next.

Her fingers trailed over his abdomen. "Do you work out?" Her voice was soft and slightly out of breath.

"Occasionally." His voice was strained. "Sweetheart," he said against her ear as her fingers slid between his skin and the fabric of his pants. "Let's take this into the bedroom." He didn't give her time to answer before he swept her into his arms and carried her down the short hallway.

Dani felt delicate in his embrace. She always thought she was a little too heavy for a man to pick up, but with Gabriel, he did it so effortlessly, she didn't mind at all. The bedroom was lit by the moonlight coming through the glass windows. She saw the bed, and the next thing she knew, she was on the mattress. He stood beside the bed and stripped off the rest of his clothing.

Dani reached down to remove her pants, but Gabriel stopped her with a look.

"That's my job," he said with a husky whisper, desire

in his voice.

A shiver worked its way up her spine. This was going to be a fun night. She could feel it in her bones. Lying back, she put her hands at her sides and waited. Gabriel nodded and moved to the end of the bed before he crawled onto the mattress.

His knees framed her ankles as he reached up and hooked his fingers into the waistband of her pants. In less than a minute, her pants and underwear were gone. His hands roamed up her body to her breasts and tunneled under her back. She wasn't sure how he managed it, but he removed her T-shirt while she was lying flat on the bed. He tossed it aside. Good thing she hadn't worn a bra.

His cock pulsed against her skin. Hard and needy. Dani licked her lips. Would he taste any different than he had years ago?

"I can see the wheels turning in your head." He leaned down until their foreheads touched. "Maybe later you can suck me off, but right now…" He closed his eyes and opened them. Hot flames of desire burned in his eyes. "Right now, I want this to be good for you."

Dani couldn't breathe. The hunger flowing through her made her forget everything. When Gabriel's hands slid inside her knees, Dani opened her legs to him. Excitement and want flowed through her veins. She wanted this. She wanted Gabriel. Even if it didn't last.

* * * *

Gabriel was pleased to see the slight flush on Dani's skin. Her breathing had increased. This felt so right. The two of them. It had always felt right. All his doubts about the past and the future flew away. There would be time to think about that later. Right now, all he could think of was Dani.

She made him feel powerful and humble at the same time. She'd placed so much trust in him, and he wasn't going to make a mistake and rush her like he had in college. She hadn't experienced a good D/s relationship. He was going to enjoy introducing her to new pleasures. To his pleasure.

He crawled between her open legs, allowing her body to cradle his. He leaned over and kissed her nipples, one at a time. They begged for attention. He would give it to them. Her hands gripped his shoulders.

"Not yet, sweetheart. I want you to put your hands at your sides and keep them there." He kept his tone soft, but it was still commanding.

"Yes…Sir."

While he was pleased that she called him sir, it wasn't what he wanted tonight. "It's just Dani and Gabriel tonight."

Their gazes met, and she nodded. Gabriel pressed a kiss between her breasts before kissing his way to the top of her mound. Her hips shifted, and he had to bite back a grin. She was impatient, something that hadn't changed.

Balancing on his knees, Gabriel ran a finger over her slit. A moan escaped Dani's lips. He dipped his finger in her and pulled it out. She was wet. Good, but he was still going to take this at his pace. He shifted his body until his shoulders were braced against her inner thighs, tilting her pelvis. Using his fingers, he parted her labia and licked her.

Honey and cream. Dani had always had her own unique taste. Maybe it was because she had such a bright and sunny personality. It was time for them to reconnect on a primal level. He speared his tongue into her pussy. Her guttural moan made him smile.

He raised his gaze and stared up at her. Her breathing

was more rapid now, and the slight flush on her body had turned a deep rose color. He continued to use his tongue and lips until her hips began to wiggle.

"Please," she said in a breathless voice. "I need to touch you. Please let me touch you."

Gabriel lifted his head. "You may touch me now." He dropped his head right back down and continued to torment her with his tongue and lips.

Her fingers tangled in his hair, cradling him against her. "It's been too long," she whispered.

He wondered what she meant by that. She'd been playing at a club and at parties in San Francisco. Was it possible a Dom never went down on her? She said she hadn't had sex with her Dom, but certainly there had been some physical contact between them or others.

Her pussy contracted. She was still super sensitive, and that wasn't a bad thing. Moving his hand from her hip, his thumb brushed over her clit.

Her hips bucked. At least he'd been prepared for that.

"Keep that up, and I'll come right now."

That was the point. He doubled his efforts. He wanted her to come. He wanted to give her pleasure, and he wanted to watch her come apart from his mouth. Her moans were music to his ears as he continued to bring her closer and closer to the edge.

Her legs curled around his back, and her fingers tightened in his scalp. It was time. Time to take her over that edge. With his thumb, he applied just the right pressure to her clit, and Dani cried out as her body shook beneath him.

Sweet honey cream flowed over his tongue. Her breathy moans continued as shivers wracked her body. After a minute or so, her legs fell away, and her fingers released his head.

Gabriel lifted his head and rested his cheek on her stomach as he gazed up at her. Her chest rose and fell rapidly, and her mouth was open, as she gulped air. But her eyes were closed. Slowly, he kissed his way up to her jaw and paused to imprint this picture of her passion.

Her lashes fluttered, and her eyes opened. There was contentment and desire in her eyes. He smiled. She looked well satisfied.

"Wipe that triumphant grin from your face." There was laughter in her voice.

"Make me." He'd missed this, the times where they would joke around after making love. That's what this was, making love. He couldn't help how he felt. Her reaction to his touch, to his mouth, and to him made him silly with happiness.

"Maybe later." Her eyes closed. "Right now, I can barely think."

"That's not a bad thing." Gabriel rolled to his side and pulled Dani with him. His cock throbbed, but he ignored it. "Rest. There's more to come later." He cradled her in his arms.

She relaxed against him. Several minutes later, she was asleep. He didn't mind. He glanced over at the small digital clock on the nightstand. 2:00 a.m. No wonder she was tired.

Keeping her in his arms, he managed to pull the sheet over them. He settled against his pillows. He'd let her sleep. They had time. More than enough time. Because he wasn't letting her go. Not now, not ever.

* * * *

Dani woke the next morning with a smile on her face. She was lying on Gabriel's chest, and his hair tickled her cheek. She enjoyed it. At one point, for a half-second, she

113

started to panic. What was this relationship going to do to both of them? She pushed the thought aside. This wasn't the time to think about a future with Gabriel. If she had one.

She just wanted to lie there and bask in the warmth and the feel of his body beneath hers. Last night felt different from when they'd been together before. Probably because they were older and wiser now. Dani giggled. She wasn't so sure about the wiser.

"So, you're awake." Gabriel's husky voice made her smile widen.

She tilted her head to see Gabriel staring down at her. "Good morning."

"It is since I have you in my arms."

Her body heated at his words. But there was a more pressing matter she needed to deal with. "If you'll excuse me, Mother Nature calls." She wiggled out of his hold and sat up on the edge of the bed. Where were her clothes?

Lord only knew. Dani let the sheet fall from her body. It wasn't as if Gabriel hadn't seen her naked before. She crossed the room and slipped into the bathroom, shutting the door behind her. She used the facilities and was washing her hands when she looked at herself in the mirror.

She had some beard burn on her neck. After she dried her hands, she looked at the rest of her body. No other marks. But what had she expected? They hadn't done a scene last night. Turning to open the bathroom door, she spied Gabriel's robe. She grabbed it and slipped it on.

When she stepped out of the bathroom, Gabriel was slipping on a pair of sweatpants. She stopped in her tracks to appreciate the muscles flexing in his back as he moved "I hope you don't mind that I borrowed your robe."

Gabriel turned to face her. His sweats didn't hide much. His hard cock strained against the material. "Looks better on you than it ever did on me." He turned and bent over to pick up their clothes off the floor and set them on the bed. "We were kind of messy last night."

"I think you mean you were messy."

"True. But you tasted so good."

Heat swept through her. This man could render her speechless so easily. But now what? She wasn't sure what to do. It wasn't like she and Gabriel hadn't woken up together before. But this felt different. This was different.

"I can see you thinking." Gabriel strode over to her and put his hands on her shoulders. "Let's have breakfast, and then we can chat."

"I think I'd like that." Breakfast. She wasn't so sure about the chat. But they did need to talk. He'd given her such pleasure last night but hadn't let her return it. That wasn't unusual for him, but it still surprised her that Gabriel could be so thoughtful. Most men weren't.

Dani followed him to his kitchen, and the smell of fresh coffee hit her senses. "When did you have time to start coffee?" She spied the full pot sitting on the counter.

Gabriel chuckled. "It's on a timer." He pulled two mugs from the cabinet and poured the coffee. "Go sit down at the table while I get creamer out of the refrigerator."

She picked up both mugs and carried them to the nice, heavy wooden table. "Where did you get this?" She ran her hand over the polished tabletop.

"One of the guys at the club does woodworking in his spare time." He set the cream in front of her and pushed the sugar bowl over. "You like cream and sugar with your coffee."

"I do." What else did he remember? She added the cream and sugar and took a sip. A moan left her lips. "Ahh, that first sip always tastes so good."

He didn't say anything, and when Dani glanced at him, he was watching her, his deep brown eyes thoughtful.

"What did you want to talk about?" Now why did she ask that?

"Tell me more about the time you spent at the clubs and parties in San Francisco."

Dani looked down at her coffee cup. "What more is there to tell?"

"Dani." His voice dropped, and a tiny shiver went through her body. "What are you not telling me?"

"What makes you think I haven't told you something?" Oh dear Lord, was she that transparent? Her stomach clenched as the icy fingers of deception crept up her spine.

"The woman I had in my bed last night said it'd been too long. At first, that didn't make sense to me, but in the light of day, I have to wonder. I know you didn't have sex with your Dom, but you must have had sex with other people."

She curled her fingers around the warm mug, seeking its heat. "Of course I did." That was a lie. She peeked from beneath her lashes to see Gabriel staring at her.

"Now why don't I believe that." He cradled his mug in his hands as he sat back in the chair. "I haven't been a saint, but there hasn't been a parade of women in my life either. So how many men did you sleep with?"

Part of her wanted to lie, and another part reminded her if this relationship was to work, they needed to be open and honest with each other. She almost snorted. "There were two men. I dated both for a while, and we had sex. That was it."

"How long has it been since you last orgasmed?"

"Last night," she quipped.

"I guess I walked into that one. Before last night."

She took another sip of her coffee and calculated the time. Oh this was so bad, so very bad. "Why is this so important to you?"

His coffee mug hit the table with a clunk. Gabriel leaned forward, elbows on the table, fingers steepled, his chin resting on his thumbs. "Communication, remember. Last night your reactions were of a woman who hadn't had pleasure in a very long time. I want to know what I'm dealing with."

"It's been two years since the last boyfriend, and I don't know, four and a half years since I last orgasmed." She kept her gaze on him, watching him calculate the time in his head.

"Are you telling me the last time you climaxed was with me in college?"

Dani gathered her courage. "Yep."

Storm clouds gathered in Gabriel's eyes as he pushed back from the table and stormed into the kitchen. Dani didn't move. The clanging of pans let her know that Gabriel was having trouble processing what she said.

He'd been like that when they were together. Whenever he got angry and couldn't process his thoughts, he'd go to the kitchen and cook. She called it his stress reliever. Dani drank the rest of her coffee, and went to stand in the doorway to the kitchen.

Gabriel was transferring items from the refrigerator to the counter. A carton of eggs, a slab of bacon, cheese, and a bowl of fruit.

"Do you want a bacon and cheese omelet, or would you rather have everything separate?" he asked with his back to her.

"Whatever's easiest for you." He didn't answer her, just started breaking and whipping up eggs. "Gabriel…"

she started.

"Since college, Dani? Since me?" His tone was soft, but there was something else—almost like pain.

She wanted to be flippant about it, but she found she couldn't. Striding across the room, she slipped her arms around his waist and hugged him from behind. "They didn't do it for me. I couldn't let go of my control with them."

"But you had no trouble with me last night."

"No, I didn't." She wasn't surprised. Gabriel had a way of taking over her body and her senses. A technique to allow her to let go of her control and accept her body's wants and needs.

"I…" Gabriel's hands covered hers where she hugged him. "That's a heavy responsibility."

"It's not your responsibility." She wasn't going to let him take this on his shoulders.

"I wasn't your Dom in college, but I am now. It is my responsibility to make sure you have pleasure."

"And it's my responsibility to make sure you have your pleasure." He wasn't going to get away with a double standard in their relationship. Not if they were going to have one. "Last night, you gave me pleasure but didn't allow me to give you any."

Gabriel stepped back from the counter, forcing her to take several steps back. He turned in her embrace and looked down at her. "My pleasure came from yours."

She framed his face with her hands. "And that was fine. But know this, I might be submissive in the bedroom and in the club, but outside of those two, I'm in control of my life. That's a hard limit for me. You are not to take responsibility for me."

He looked down at her. "You're right." His body relaxed under her touch. "I was just so surprised. You're so sensual. While we were together, you never ever had an issue with your body or having sex."

"I was much freer in college. Now, I have huge responsibilities. The business and my grandparents."

Gabriel lowered his head until his forehead rested against hers. "Will you at least share those burdens with me?"

"Only if you share yours."

"Done." He smiled. "Now, if you'll stop molesting me, I can get us breakfast."

"Molesting you?" It was laughter in her voice. She'd missed this. Dani released him and moved to the other side of the kitchen. She loved watching Gabriel cook.

* * * *

Gabriel took a deep breath as he cooked the bacon. He hadn't expected Dani's words, and while his masculine side preened, his Dom side cringed. Yes, he'd brought her pleasure last night, but this was a woman who had been without pleasure for over four years.

He quickly finished cooking, and they ate. "What do you have on tap for today?"

"I need to go check on my grandparents and go into the office for a little bit. There are a few things I need to go over when no one's around."

"May I come with you?" He wanted to see her grandparents, but he was curious about her office. Also, he didn't want her to be alone. Yes, he was being overprotective, and he knew it. But he just couldn't turn off that side of himself.

"If you want. And, before I forget, I have training on the new computer system at the club tomorrow." She pushed her empty breakfast plate away. "That was absolutely delicious. Thank you."

"You're very welcome. I'll clean the kitchen while you get dressed." He picked up the empty plates. "I'm assuming you want to go to your apartment and change before you go to your grandparents."

Twin suns appeared on her cheeks, and Gabriel bit back a grin. "I probably should."

Gabriel watched Dani saunter to his bedroom. His heart was light. This was where Dani belonged. With him and in his life. He carried the dishes into the kitchen and rinsed them off to load them into the dishwasher.

There was still something that bugged him about the way they broke up in college. But now was not the time to talk about it. They were just getting back on even footing, and right now, Dani was talking to him.

Had he ever stopped loving her? He doubted it. That's partly why he'd stayed in contact with her grandparents. Any little news of her made his heart shine.

Gabriel shook his head. He hadn't thought this long and hard about a relationship ever. He wasn't one to wax poetic. Dani brought that out and him. He finished cleaning the kitchen and walked toward the bedroom. Dani was finished, so he took a quick shower and dressed. Soon, they were on their way to her apartment.

Chapter 7

Dani pulled into the Wicked Sanctuary parking lot Thursday evening. Gabriel had reminded her earlier today that he was giving a demonstration tonight. She wondered why he hadn't mentioned it before now and hadn't told her what to wear. Excitement thrummed through her. Tonight, they would play in the club.

She smiled at Ralph as she signed in. It would be interesting to see how many people showed up for this demo. After she changed and went into the club, she found Sierra and Rose talking by the bar.

"Nice outfit," Rose commented.

"Thanks." Dani had chosen a black lace top along with a thong. She wanted to be ready for whatever Gabriel planned for tonight. She looked around the club. There he was. "If you'll excuse me, I need to make sure I'm dressed okay for Gabriel."

Gabriel looked up from the scene he was setting up as she approached. "Good evening, Sir."

"Good evening, Dani." His gaze took in what she was wearing and desire flared in his eyes. "When the scene is done, I'm going to take you home and torment you."

Her body heated, and a flush went from her toes to her head. "Didn't you do that Saturday?"

Gabriel laughed. "Did you dress this way just for me?"

"I did. But I wasn't sure how you wanted me dressed for this demo."

Gabriel blinked, and his face went blank. "For the

demo?"

"Yes, Sir." Dani shifted from one foot to the other. Why was Gabriel so reluctant? "You do want me to be the sub in your demo, don't you?"

Gabriel stepped off the small stage and put his hands on Dani's shoulders. "I'm sorry. I forgot about it until Max called me. I don't think we're a good fit for this demo."

Dani stiffened and just stared at Gabriel. "Why not?" She was trying to keep the anger out of her voice.

"We've only been playing together a short time, and we need to understand more about each other before doing this." He waved at the stage.

"What does that have to do with anything? Am I your sub or not?"

"You are, but you will not be my demo sub tonight." His fingers tightened on her shoulders. "I should have said something to you earlier, and I didn't. That was my mistake."

Her anger boiled up. "I guess this means you're no longer my Dom." She shrugged his hands away and turned.

"Dani." He reached out and grabbed her elbow.

"No. You can't have it both ways. You told me you would discuss it with me, and you didn't. So I guess that means I'm not your sub." She pulled her arm away and marched back over to the bar. Sierra and Rose were a little out of focus.

"Oh, Dani…" Sierra put her arm around Dani's shoulder and guided her to one of the sofas.

"Was I wrong to assume that I would be his sub tonight?" Dani hated the wobble in her voice. Gabriel was rejecting her. It hurt so much.

"I don't think so," Rose said, sitting down across from them.

"You and Gabriel have a history. Could it be that history that's making him hesitate?" Sierra asked.

Dani shook her head. "It shouldn't. We've talked. We know each other's limits. Why won't he talk to me?"

Sierra frowned. "Well, something is holding him back."

"I don't know what, and he won't tell me. I know one thing. He broke his word to me."

* * * *

Gabriel watched Dani march away. He had no idea what to do.

"I see you don't learn from your mistakes," Zeke said.

Gabriel shook his head. "I can't use her as my demo sub."

"Why the hell not? Is spanking and the use of paddles a hard limit for her?"

"No. But I'm going to use some impression toys tonight; those are hard limits for her." He glanced over where Dani sat with Sierra and Rose. Dani wasn't ready for this.

"You're careful with impression toys. You never leave a mark beyond a few minutes." Zeke stared at him. "Talk with her. Tell her that you'll need to use another sub for the impression toys if they're a hard limit. But I sense there's something else."

"I won't use her. I will not scare her." Not again. Never again.

"Have you told her this?" Zeke asked.

Gabriel shook his head.

"You're being a fool. Dani isn't going to accept a half-assed Dom. So if that's how you're going to act, she is right to walk away."

Gabriel opened his mouth to reply when Max approach

them. "Why is Dani sitting with Sierra and Rose? Shouldn't you be getting her ready?"

"He's not using Dani," Zeke commented.

"What?" Max stared at Gabriel. "After all the crap around you two getting together, you're not going to use her?"

"Listen Max, this is really between Dani and me." Damn. He screwed up. He needed to talk to Dani and sort this out. Now. He took a step in her direction until Max stopped him cold with his words.

"This is my club, and Dani is one of my people. So either you tell me what's going on, or I'll get the story out of Dani."

Gabriel rubbed his forehead. "Apologies, Max. I know you're just looking out for everyone in the club. Dani has a hard limit with impression toys, and this demo was set up before we got together. Plus, I made the mistake of not telling her beforehand."

"I see. But spanking and paddles are not a hard limit," Max said.

"No, but impression paddles are. And I'm using one of those tonight."

Max frowned. "I see. Have you told her you can use the impression paddle without leaving an impression?"

Zeke snorted. "He's too wrapped up in his own head. He won't use her."

"I don't want to scare her." Gabriel shifted on his feet. He really was looking after Dani, no matter what anyone else thought.

"You have a choice, Gabriel. You have five minutes to ask Dani if she wants to be your sub for the demo and explain you're using an impression toy. Give her a choice. If she says no, no foul. If she says yes, and you refuse, you do it with the knowledge you can never approach her in the club again."

Gabriel stared at Max. "You're joking, right?"

"Do I look like I am?"

Gabriel saw the determination and finality in Max's eyes. Was Gabriel wrong? It wouldn't be the first time. Why did he seem to screw things up with Dani? Because he cared. He cared a lot. He worked hard to make sure she was comfortable, to the point of not telling her things that he deemed uncomfortable for her. Another damn mistake.

Without a word, he walked away from the two men and over to where Dani sat with Sierra and Rose. "My apologies." He held his hand out to her. "We need to talk before I do the demo."

"Are you going to allow me to be your demo sub?"

"Depends on your answers. Honest answers."

"All right." She placed her hand in his.

He helped Dani stand and guided her over to the scene area. "Let's discuss what I'm going to do tonight." This is what he should have done before they came to the club. Or at least told her they needed to talk when she got here. But when she said she was ready to be his sub, he retreated to an old pattern of non-explanation instead. He would break that habit, even if it killed him.

"You will be restrained over a spanking horse. I will start with a light spanking, move on to using a flogger, a paddle, and lastly, I will be using an impression paddle."

Her eyes widened. "May I see the impression paddle?"

Gabriel reached over and plucked the paddle from where he'd placed it earlier. It was pretty good size, made of leather with holes in it. Dani took a deep breath when he held it out to her. Her fingers trembled when she took it from him.

He watched as she ran her fingers over the leather and the holes. Her breathing had increased, and he wasn't sure if it was fear or excitement.

"Tell me about the marks you'll leave."

"Any marks I leave will be temporary; they will disappear in a few minutes."

"And pain?"

"Momentary. I don't want a sub in pain; this is all about pleasure." He took a deep breath. "We can do this a couple of ways. You can be my demo sub for everything but the impression paddle, for the entire scene, or not at all. It's up to you." He braced himself for the rejection.

She handed him the paddle. "Who will you use the impression paddle on?"

"Hannah. She agreed when I first set up this demo." Gabriel put the paddle back on the table and stared at her. Her eyes were clear, no fear but no excitement either.

"Be right back." Dani walked over to where Hannah stood. He watched as they two chatted, they both laughed.

"Okay," Dani announced when she returned to him. "Hannah understands you'll use me for the first part, then we'll switch places. I understand you'll need to warm her up before you use the impression toy."

Gabriel blinked. "If we do this, club safe words apply."

"Agreed."

"I want you to understand the way I use an impression paddle; it won't leave any bruising or marks on Hannah."

"Yes, Sir. I trust you."

Gabriel fell back a step. Her trust floored him. "I am humbled by your trust."

Dani put her hand on his cheek. "I agreed for you to be my Dom. I didn't do it lightly. But I expect the same from you."

He closed his eyes and opened them. "I understand now. I'm sorry I didn't talk with you."

"I'm stronger than I look, Sir."

"You are." Her strength ran deep, and he needed to remember that. With a deep breath, he led her up onto the stage. "Did you dress with the idea of being my demo sub?"

"Yes, Sir."

"Go wait by the scene." He watched Dani walk away with a new admiration for her in his bones. Gabriel had a quick conversation with Hannah on how they would switch, then had a quick conversation with Zeke who would take care of Dani until he finished the scene. He guided Dani to the spanking horse as the club patrons started gathering around. If she safe-worded out when he used the implements, he knew he could trust her to know her own limits. Sometimes a sub went beyond their limits to please their Dom. He didn't want her to do that. He'd have to watch her carefully.

"Top on or off, Sir?"

"I'll leave that up to you. I only need access to your ass, and I have that."

She nodded and glanced at the spanking horse.

"I've set this one up a little different." He helped Dani lay over the top part. Her feet rested on the floor, but her top half rested on a padded shelf on the other side. "This way the audience can see what I'm doing, but you'll be somewhat comfortable." He picked up the restraints for her wrists and attached them. He checked to make sure there was room between the cuffs and her wrists so he didn't cut off circulation. Dani took a deep breath and let it out.

Gabriel moved behind her. He rubbed her ass, causing a contented murmur from Dani. He ran his hands down her thighs to her ankles, restraining each ankle one at a time.

She'd be able to rise to her toes but not much else.

Gabriel straightened and turned to the table where he'd laid out everything he needed, and glanced out into the club were the small crowd had assembled.

If this didn't go well— Gabriel shook his head to clear it. This was a demo, and he needed to get his head in the game. Now. He took a deep breath. "Good evening, everyone. I'm going to show you a bit of impact play tonight. The important thing is to warm your sub up before you get into the heavy items."

He walked over to Dani and rubbed her ass, watching her for any negative reaction and was satisfied when she didn't flinch or move.

"You don't need anything fancy at home," he explained to the audience. "You can do this with your sub bent over the sofa or even on a bed. I will say as long as you're careful, be creative. The key is to make sure your sub is comfortable but not too comfortable." Gabriel swatted her ass, and Dani squealed in surprise. He swatted her again. "It is important to rub the areas that you use impact toys on. It helps dissipate the pain but also keeps the skin sensitive. It also serves to keep you connected to your sub." He rubbed her ass, enjoying the feel of the heat his spanking caused. He gave her several more swats, stopping to rub her ass often as he talked to the audience.

"Are you doing okay?" he whispered in her ear.

"Yes, Sir." Her voice was strong and her eyes clear.

Gabriel turned and picked up one of the light floggers. Again, he talked to the audience as he flogged her, checking in with her several times. Her ass had turned a pretty shade of pink. Next, he picked up one of the paddles.

"This paddle is twofold," he said to the audience, holding it up in such a way that he knew Dani could see it too. He didn't want to surprise her. "One side is covered with soft fabric, and the other is not." He turned the soft fabric side down and swatted Dani with it.

She went up on her toes and gasped. Gabriel glanced at her, and she smiled at him and mouthed, "I'm okay."

Gabriel continued with the demo until Dani was moaning and going on her toes with almost every swat. He looked into her glazed eyes. "Impression paddle is next. Time to switch out."

"Yes, Sir."

He released the restraints, put a blanket around her, and guided her to Zeke, who ushered her to the sofa where Allyson sat so Dani could finish watching the demo. Hannah took Dani's place. Within minutes, Hannah was ready.

Gabriel walked over and picked up the impression paddle. He held the paddle up to the audience and heard some oohs and ahhs.

"This impression paddle has holes in it. How hard you use it determines how much of an impression it will leave and how long it will last. I don't believe in marking a sub for more than a few minutes. That isn't to say she won't be aware the next day of what happened."

He flicked the paddle against Hannah's ass. He glanced at Dani in the audience. Her eyes were wide, and her mouth open, but she'd leaned forward. She didn't seem afraid of what he was doing.

Gabriel's swatted her other ass cheek. It turned red, and the audience could see the impression of the paddle for just a moment before it faded.

"Okay?" he asked Hannah, rubbing her butt.

"Yes, Sir."

When the paddle came down again, it was harder.

Hannah yelped. On it went with him stopping to check in with her. Each time, she told him she was fine.

After a few more strikes, Gabriel stopped the demo. He helped Hannah up and put a blanket around her. He started to escort her to the aftercare area.

"I'm fine, Sir," Hannah said. "That was nice warm-up. Take care of Dani."

Gabriel glanced over to where Dani was sitting. Her eyes were closed, but there was a small smile on her face. He marched over to her, picked her up, and carried her in his arms over to the aftercare area, and sat down with her in his lap.

Dani curled into his embrace. He was surprised at how well she took the demo. After everything she had said, he'd been worried. More than worried. Afraid this would damage their budding relationship. But his girl took it like a champ. He was proud of her.

"Please stop worrying." Her voice was soft. When he glanced down, he saw her eyes were open— a bit unfocused, but alight with wonder.

"Was I too hard on you?"

"No. I've never felt anything like that before." Gabriel wondered what that meant. "It wasn't a bad thing, so don't start worrying. Watching you with Hannah and the impression paddle…I have to tell you: It's euphoric."

"So I've heard." He shifted her on his lap, and she moaned.

"I know I'm going to feel this tomorrow, but it's going to be a good feeling. It will remind me how you made me feel tonight."

"And how was that?" He really wanted to know what was going on inside her head.

"Wanted. Taken care of."

His heart swelled. "I will always take care of you."

* * * *

Dani laid in Gabriel's arms. His words warmed her heart. Her ass burned, but it was that good kind of burn. She didn't know how to explain it. When he'd started, the swats were soft, almost too soft, but as they progressed, the swats got harder.

Her skin tingled as the heat from the spanking flowed through her body and turned into pure pleasure. When he'd switched to Hannah, she was a little disappointed. She almost asked him to continue, but stopped. She needed to see how Gabriel handled the impression paddle. Snug in the blanket Gabriel had draped over her, Zeke led her to a seat next to Allyson so they could watch.

When Gabriel started with the impression paddle on Hannah, Dani flinched on the first hit.

While she hadn't felt the swat, she saw the impressions. Gabriel was careful, and the impressions only lasted a couple of seconds and then faded. When it ended, Dani was on the edge. Her body so hot and needy. She was lost in the sensations.

Dani snuggled deeper in his arms.

"How is she?" That was Zeke.

"Good." Gabriel said.

She was good and was enjoying being cuddled by him, so she stayed still and silent.

"I never thought I'd see the day you were committed to one woman," Zeke said.

Dani fought not to stiffen in Gabriel's arms. What was Zeke doing? He had to know Gabriel was commitment phobic.

"You know darn well, Zeke, I'll never commit to marriage."

Dani bit the inside of her cheek so as not to cry out. Gabriel wouldn't change his mind about that. Probably never would. She knew that going into this relationship, but that didn't mean it didn't hurt. She'd hoped he would see she wasn't like his mother or father. Hope died in her.

"Buddy, you need to either commit or let Dani go. It isn't fair to her," Zeke said.

"This is between Dani and me."

Dani recognized that hard tone. Gabriel was on the defensive. She wiggled in his arms.

"Be careful," Zeke said.

"Dani?"

She opened her eyes and looked at him. "Hi." The conversation she overheard was spinning in her mind. What did she expect?

"How are you doing?"

"I really am good." Or at least as good as she could be with her heart cracking open.

Gabriel gazed down at her. "Your eyes are clearer now, and your voice is steady. I'm going to go clean up the scene, but you sit here and just relax." He gently moved her to the other side of the sofa and stood. He picked up the bottle of water sitting on the table, twisted the cap loose, and handed it to her. "Drink. I'll be back in a few minutes."

Dani watched Gabriel, admiring his efficiency at cleaning up the scene and his toys. He put them back in his bag and stored the bag in the cubby by the bar. When he walked back over to her, she had finished the water. She tucked away her feelings about the conversation she'd overheard to look at later. Right now, she wanted to keep dreaming.

"I'm going to take you home now." Gabriel leaned down and lifted her into his arms.

"I can walk. My car is here; how am I going to get it?" While she appreciated his concern, she really was okay.

"I'm taking you home—there's no two ways about it." Gabriel strode toward the bar where Zeke was sitting. "Zeke, can you make sure the ladies' room is empty so I can take Dani in to get her things. And is it possible for Allyson to drive Dani's car to her place with you following?"

"No problem. We can take care of Dani's car."

Gabriel followed Zeke out of the club and into the foyer. When Zeke told him the ladies' room was empty, he carried Dani in.

"Is this really necessary?" Dani asked.

"It is for me. Which locker?"

Dani stared at Gabriel, then relented. "Third one from the left, in the middle."

Gabriel carried her over and set her on her feet, keeping one arm around her waist. She unlocked it and pulled her bag out. He took her bag, slipped the strap over his shoulder, and kept her steady as they walked out to where Zeke and Allyson were waiting.

"I don't want to ruin their night."

"You're not," Allyson said, holding her hand out for Dani's keys. "I know where you parked it."

Dani shook her head. "Why will nobody listen to me when I say I'm okay?"

"Because we want to take care of you," Zeke said. "Let us do this for you."

Dani nodded, and before she knew it, she was in Gabriel's arms once again as he carried her out of the club to his car. Once he made sure she was comfortable and belted in, he climbed in and started the car. She rested her head against the window. It was dark, so she really couldn't see much.

In what felt like record time, he pulled up in front of her apartment building. "You are not carrying me in."

"I am walking you in."

"Okay." She waited until he came around and opened her door. She'd learned that lesson early when Gabriel admonished her for not allowing him to help her out of the car. Together they made their way to her apartment. Dani was steady on her feet, her mind perfectly clear. She unlocked her door, pushed it open, and turned to Gabriel.

"Tonight was amazing. Thank you."

"I should stay with you tonight."

She shook her head. She needed time to process everything that had happened. "I'm totally fine. I'm going to undress and go to bed. Go home, Gabriel. We can talk tomorrow." She went up on her toes and brushed a kiss over his lips before stepping back and closing the door.

Dani was surprised when Gabriel walked away, but maybe he understood that she needed this time alone. He'd set her bag by the door. She left it there and padded into her bedroom. Once there, she quickly changed out of her club clothes and into a T-shirt and fell onto the bed. She was so tired.

Tomorrow would be soon enough to deal with her emotions over tonight, what she'd overheard, and to try talking with Gabriel. She wanted to enjoy the way her ass still tingled from their scene, because it was probably the last time it would ever happen.

* * * *

Gabriel was on his third cup of coffee when Zeke walked into the office.

"Did you sleep at all?" Zeke asked.

"Very little. Dani wouldn't let me stay with her, and I

haven't been able to reach her this morning." He took a hearty drink of his coffee. "I'm worried about subdrop."

"Why are you sitting here?" Zeke prompted.

Gabriel didn't waste a second. He jogged to his car and drove over to Dani's place. Her car was in its allotted slot. The lobby door was locked, and she wasn't answering her bell. He was starting to get really worried and was about to call the police department for a welfare check when someone opened the door.

The older woman looked at him suspiciously, and he put on his most charming smile. "Good morning, I was just checking on Dani. She is new in the building."

"Oh, that nice young girl." The woman stared at him. "Didn't I see you here the other night?"

"Yes. We had a date, but I haven't been able to reach her this morning, and I wanted to check on her."

The older woman stepped aside, holding the door open. "It's nice to see that you young men can be gentlemen and check on a woman."

"Yes, ma'am." It took everything in him not to run down the hallway. When he got to Dani's door, he pounded on it. "Dani," he yelled.

The door opened, and Dani stood there. The air left his lungs. She looked beautiful with mussed hair and bare feet.

"Gabriel? What are you doing here?"

"I been trying to reach you for the past few hours."

"I'm sorry." She stepped back and gestured for him to enter. She closed the door behind him. "I just woke up a few minutes ago, and my cell phone is dead. I forgot to plug it in last night."

Gabriel pulled her into his arms and held her. "I was worried."

"I can see that." She brushed a kiss over his jaw. "I'm

perfectly fine."

"I'll be the judge of that." He held her at arm's length. "I want to see your ass."

Dani burst out laughing. "My ass is just fine, thank you." She shrugged away from his hold. "Would you like some coffee? Or, better yet, food?"

Gabriel stared at her. "I'm not joking here. I need to make sure everything is okay."

Dani returned his stare with one of her own and shrugged. "Fine." She turned her back to him and lowered the shorts she was wearing.

Gabriel walked over and ran his hand over her luscious ass. No welts, no bruising. Good. Dani shivered, and Gabriel couldn't help himself, he gave her a light swat on her ass.

Dani moaned. "More, please, Sir."

Gabriel closed his eyes against the temptation to do what she wanted. But when she pushed her ass into his hands, common sense went out the window. He flipped her around in his arms and lifted her onto his shoulder.

"Gabriel!" she said, laughing.

He marched into her bedroom and sat on the rumpled covers of her bed. He flipped her around until she was over his lap. He gave her several quick spanks, before he sat her down next to him. "Don't be a brat."

"I like being a brat." She leaned over and covered his lips with hers.

Gabriel allowed her to take control of the kiss. Just this once, he'd allow it. He enjoyed the feeling of her soft lips against his, the way her tongue slipped into his mouth and played with his. When she lifted her head, he couldn't stop grinning. "You do realize that you might be playing with fire."

"Let's stoke the fire."

Gabriel stood and stared down at her. "You have five seconds to strip, or I'll rip those clothes off of you."

Her eyes widened, but she stood, kicked off her shorts, and pulled off the T-shirt she was wearing. "Where do you want me, Sir?"

"Let's have a little fun." Gabriel stripped out of his clothes and climbed onto the mattress. "Come ride me."

Her eyes lit up like fourth July, then she was poised over him. "Condom?"

He groaned. He hadn't expected to have sex with her this morning. "I don't have one. You caught me by surprise."

"Good thing I'm prepared." She stretched out and opened the nightstand drawer. She pulled out a box and plucked a foil square out of it.

"We'll talk later about why you have a box of condoms next to your bed."

"Of course, Sir." She ripped the package open. "But just so you know, I bought these two days ago. I'll even show you the receipt."

Gabriel opened his mouth, but nothing came out as she rolled the protection over his pulsing dick. He grasped her hips as she positioned herself over him.

Their gazes collided, and she lowered herself onto him. His cock was encased by her warm, wet heat. She moaned as she took more of him inside her pussy.

Once he was fully inside her , she rose up and down. Gabriel kept his hands on her hips, to guide and support her. Over and over. Up and down in exquisite torture. It was all too soon that Dani cried out as she climaxed. And Gabriel followed right behind her.

Dani collapsed on top of him, and he gently settled her

to his side before he got up to take care of the condom. When he returned to the bed, she was already asleep. Gabriel climbed into bed and pulled the covers over them. A short nap would do them both good.

* * * *

Dani moved around her kitchen as quietly as she could and looked in the fridge. What would work for a late lunch? She'd already downed a cup of coffee but needed food. Dani stared at the contents. Not much there, but she had eggs, cheese, and bread for toast.

She'd left Gabriel asleep in bed. The poor guy had admitted to not getting much sleep last night. Now, it was almost one in the afternoon.

Her cell beeped, and she paused to look at it. Yesterday, before she left work, she'd given her crews their assignments for today and told them she was taking the day off. It was unusual for her, but she was sure that after the demo last night, she wouldn't be in any shape to work today. The text was from one of her workers to let her know they'd just finished another job. She texted back, *Great job*.

There were no other messages to deal with, so she resumed preparing the brunch. Cracking the eggs into a bowl, she beat them and poured the mixture into a pan. Even if Gabriel didn't wake up soon, the smell of coffee, toast and eggs might get him moving.

"Coffee?" Gabriel's sleepy voice floated over to her.

Dani turned her head. "Still warm, on the counter." She nodded to the pot.

"Thank goodness." He padded over, wearing just his jeans.

"I though you said you'd had several cups this morning?" She scrambled the eggs and added the cheese.

"I did, but I need more to get through the afternoon."

He leaned against the counter, watching her. "Breakfast?"

"Eggs with cheese and toast. That's about all I have. I need to go grocery shopping."

"Works for me. Toaster?"

"Cabinet to your left." She concentrated on the eggs while Gabriel made the toast. It was like they were back in college and they cooked at his apartment.

Dani set two plates of eggs on the table and filled two glasses with water before sitting down. Gabriel joined her. They didn't talk much as they ate.

"This feels right," Gabriel said when he finished.

"Us eating together?" She tilted her head as she watched him.

"Yes, but being together too."

Dani hid a smile. It did feel right. But after what he said last night, she wasn't sure if she was ready to trust her heart to Gabriel once again. Who was she kidding? Her heart was already involved. "Last night was great, and I can't wait for it to happen again."

His eyes widened. "Last night, I went easy on you."

"Oh." While her ass still stung a little, she was surprised he'd gone easy on her.

"Dani, last night worked out, but it might not always work out like that."

Her mouth dropped open. "It will if you talk to me."

"There's always a chance I will be asked to do another demo with a different impression paddle, and I won't be able to switch out subs. I won't hurt you."

"You didn't hurt me last night." What the hell was wrong with him?

"I was being super careful."

"With me or Hannah?" She crossed her arms over her breasts.

"In a way, both of you."

"Why?" Was that why the impression on Hannah's skin only lasted a few seconds?

"It didn't feel right to me. It was a mistake to use you that way."

"Really?" Dani took a breath to try and avoid a sarcastic comeback. "Why do you feel it was mistake?"

"It just was."

She stared at him. She knew an excuse when she heard one. "I know I reacted badly in college, and I explained why." Well, not everything.

"I expected you to safeword out last night."

Dani's mouth dropped open. "I didn't."

"No. But—"

"There is no but." She wasn't going to let him get away with this. "I enjoyed what you did last night, and you had to be aware of that." Anger was growing within her.

He nodded, but his features tightened.

"I was more than aroused by what you did to me and Hannah." She'd felt hot and tingling.

"How long did it last?"

"Until this morning." Her body still tingled when she moved just right.

"Which is why you should have let me stay with you last night." He pushed away from the table and paced around her small kitchen. "Did you feel scared or weepy last night?"

"No." She kept her gaze on him as if she would be able to see what he was thinking.

"From what you've told me, you've never been spanked the way I did last night. Damn it, Dani. Why did you push me away last night?" He pulled a hand through his hair.

"Because I knew you'd overreact, just like you're doing right now." She stood and carried their empty plates to the sink. "I was fine last night. I came home, fell asleep, and didn't wake until I heard you pounding on my door."

"How did you feel when you woke up?"

"A little disoriented." She wouldn't lie to him. "But it disappeared."

"How did your ass feel?"

A smile played around her lips. "It tingled. It wasn't sore or anything. But I remembered everything you did last night, and I want that again."

Gabriel shook his head. "It's too soon."

"I don't get this," she said, hands on hips. "Why are you being so bull headed about this? You spanked me this morning."

"Because I don't want you to hate me."

Dani blinked. "What? I could never hate you." Where was that coming from?

"You hated me in college."

"I did not." She walked over to him. "Gabriel, what's really going on? I never hated you. We wanted different things at the time. My emotional state wasn't the best, but that wasn't your fault."

"You barely talked to me before graduation."

She dipped her head. "You're right. I didn't, but not because of you." How could she explain? The only way was to tell him the truth and let the cards fall where they might. "Come into the living room." She took his hand, led him into the other room, and pushed him down on the sofa before sitting next to him.

Dani took a deep breath. "The day you talked about spanking me, I'd just gotten some very unexpected news."

"You never said anything."

"I didn't. And that wasn't right. But I was trying to deal with it, and I pretty much shut down on you. That wasn't right."

"It wasn't because I was trying to introduce kink?"

She shook her head. "Do you remember the few days prior to that night?"

Gabriel's forehead wrinkled. "We were both super busy with classes, and finals were coming up."

"Right. Do you remember I thought I had the flu?"

"Yes. You wouldn't see me for several days." He took her hands in his. "What does that have to do with it? Were you sick?"

"Not sick." She pressed her lips together, and took one breath and then another to prepare herself for her next words. "I felt really bad one morning, and my period started, or at least that's what I thought it was." The words were hard to get out. "I was in class when I doubled over with cramps. My instructor took me to the ER." Her eyes filled with tears. "I was pregnant and didn't even know it."

Gabriel sat back. The shock on his face wasn't surprising. "Pregnant." He stared at her. "How? I mean, we took precautions."

"Not always."

"Why didn't you tell me?"

"I didn't know how." She shook her head. "The shock of losing our baby hit me hard. I barely got through my finals. I didn't want you to suffer as well. You had your life planned out." She also knew how he felt about commitment.

"And you didn't have yours planned out?" He stood up and began pacing the room. "I should have been there for you."

"Maybe."

He whirled around. "What do you mean, maybe?"

"Be honest with me. You were already backing away from me, and you told me from the beginning you weren't a commitment type of guy."

"I wasn't. I'm not. You know how I feel about that."

"I do. When I thought about it, I didn't want you to think I got pregnant on purpose to force you to marry me. I would never do that."

He ran his hand over his face. "I wouldn't have thought that."

"Really?" She stared at him. "You were the one who told me you'd broken up with several girlfriends because they wanted more than you could give. While I lost our baby, I wanted it, but I also didn't want to force you to choose, so I kept silent. You would have run—hard and fast—had I told you."

"You don't know that.

"I do. Gabriel, I watched you each time you came home from a dinner with one of your parents. You were cold and distant. And you never took me with you."

"I was protecting you. You should have told me about the baby."

"Maybe. But I didn't. I was barely coping, and when you sprang kink on me, I lost it."

"If you had told me, I would have understood."

"Like you did when I freaked out about the kink? Be honest with yourself. You weren't committed to me anymore than you are now."

"What the hell? I am committed to you."

"Are you?" Dani took a deep breath and plunged on. "I heard you talking with Zeke last night. You told him you could never be committed to one woman."

Gabriel opened his mouth and then shut it. "I did, but I

didn't mean you."

"Who did you mean? We were already seeing each other again and playing in the club." He didn't deny it. Dani's heart grew heavy. "You said it yourself. You still don't believe in commitment. And I want that. With you. Maybe us getting back together wasn't such a good idea."

His features flattened out and went dead, spearing Dani's heart with knives of pain. He didn't love her. Or, if he did, it wasn't enough.

"Maybe it wasn't." Gabriel stood and walked into the bedroom. When he returned, he was dressed, his face still an emotionless mask. Dani's heart pounded. Gabriel had shut down again. He was going to leave her, not fight for her. She'd caused it, but darn it. If she meant anything to him, he'd stay and talk this out.

She stood up.

"What does this mean?" she asked.

He marched to the front door and turned back to stare at her. "I need to think." Before she could ask him how long he needed, Gabriel was gone.

Dani sank back onto the sofa, her heart hurting along with her soul. She hadn't been sure how Gabriel would take learning about the baby, but now she knew. A sigh escaped her lips. Last night had been so beautiful for both of them. Now, she wasn't sure they even had a future together.

Chapter 8

Dani walked around Max and Sierra's backyard. Her work was almost complete thanks to her crew and a run of perfect weather. The new trees and flowers complemented the layout. She checked her list as she walked over the brick pathway to the club. The last of the privacy bushes, hedges, and trees were being put in. She'd picked fast growing ones.

While she was proud of her work, she was tired. She'd worked flat out this past week. Mainly because Gabriel was avoiding her. She hadn't seen him on the job site or at the club. The frustration was beginning to wear on her.

"Hey, Dani," Max said as he rounded the corner. "I was hoping to catch you."

"What's up?"

"I was wondering if you could help out at the club tomorrow night?"

"Thursday?" The beginning of the week had flown. Probably because she wanted it to slow down.

Allyson had asked her about coming to the club when they had lunch yesterday, but she'd brushed it off, saying Gabriel was busy and she was tired. She wasn't sure her friend believed her.

"Yes. Anthony Payne is doing a demo, and a lot of members have signed up to see it."

Dani vaguely remembered seeing it on the club calendar. "Sure, I can help out. Anthony's doing a demo with knives?"

"Yes, he's a master with them. The members have been asking for a demo for a long time."

"That will be interesting." Her mood improved. She'd love to watch knife play. While they were a hard limit, she'd had some notes around knife play. Mainly she wanted to watch first and decide for herself if she wanted to try it. She was curious about how Anthony used them. "Do you want me there at seven-thirty?"

"Actually, can you be here at seven? I think people are going to show up early."

"Sure. Anything else?"

Max stared at her. "Yes. Are you okay?"

"Fine." She looked down at her clipboard.

"Dani." Max's voice was soft. "If you need to talk, I'm here."

She lifted her head. "Thanks. It will be okay." She smiled, but Max shook his head as he walked away. Her phone beeped, and she pulled it out. The last delivery for the job over at the Andersons' had arrived. One more thing to cross off her list.

* * * *

Dani shifted from one foot to the other when Anthony took the stage. She'd gotten a good look at all the items he'd brought. Who knew so many things could be involved?

Allyson grabbed her hand. "Come sit down; Lara saved us space." Allyson pulled Dani around the group and to one of the sofas at the front. She patted the empty cushion, and they sat down. Zeke and Colby sat on stools behind the sofa.

"Tonight, I'm going to talk about knife play," Anthony said. "I want to tell you: I don't draw blood. That's not what knife play is about for me. Not about cutting or pain, just pleasure. It's about the sensation of running different types of implements across one's skin."

Dani sat forward, intrigued.

* * * *

Gabriel walked into the club, feeling out of sorts. He wanted to blame it on dinner with his father, who talked about his upcoming marriage, number six, to his latest girlfriend. He shook his head; the dinner had seemed to go forever.

He wanted to get to the club and see Anthony Payne's demo. Payne was a master with the knives, and while Gabriel didn't choose to play with knives, he appreciated Payne's artistry. Gabriel also knew Dani wouldn't be there because knives were on her hard limit list.

What was he going to do about Dani? His father had droned on and on tonight about how, if this marriage didn't work on, he'd move on again. Gabriel didn't want to turn out like his parents, marriage after marriage. Yet he had to wonder if it would be different with Dani.

He shook his head. No sense in taking the chance. In the end, if he couldn't commit to one woman, he didn't want Dani to hate him. He'd rather end it now than have that. Hell, she probably hated him now.

Taking a deep breath, he slipped into the club, surprised by the number of people there. He had to move around the crowd to find a decent view.

"Anyone else from the audience like to try?" Payne asked.

Damn, he'd missed most of the demo. Oh well, there would be another time. Plus, he was sure Payne would stay around and answer questions. Several hands shot up, and Payne looked around, and said, "You" and pointed to someone sitting in front.

It wasn't until he saw the woman mount the stage his heart stopped. Dani? Knives? Shit. He took step forward. A hand on his arm stopped him. Gabriel looked up at Max.

"Let go. Knives are on her hard limits list."

"I know, but she chose to do this." Max tightened his hold. "Let her be, Gabriel."

"But—"

"Nothing. This is about Dani's needs. If she wants to be part of the demo, she can be. She knows her limits."

"I'm her Dom."

"Oh?" Max stared down at him with a hard gaze. "You didn't show up here Saturday night, and tonight, you didn't come in until just a few minutes ago. Plus, the way Dani is looking, you haven't been taking care of her like a Dom should."

"What is between Dani and me is our business."

"Until it spills over into my club." He leaned down and got into Gabriel's face. "Do you know Sierra found Dani crying while she was working in our yard this week?"

"What?" Damn, he never meant to hurt her like that. One more reason to stay away; he was hurting her.

"Dani refused to say anything, but she's been putting in long days. Our yard never looked better, but I want you to really look at Dani."

Gabriel's gaze went to the stage. Dani was there but wasn't. Her eyes were dull, and she looked tired. Really tired. Damn it. "I was late because I had dinner with my father."

Max grimaced. "Sorry. I know that's rough."

Gabriel kept one eye on Dani. He wanted to go to her, but did he have the right?

* * * *

Dani couldn't believe she'd volunteered to be part of

148

the demo. Yes, knives were a hard limit, and they still made her nervous. Even so, after watching Anthony with other subs, she had to experience this for herself.

"You're scared," Anthony whispered as she sat down on the hard chair.

"Yes, Sir." She wouldn't lie.

"Are you certain you want to do this?"

"Yes, Sir." Maybe this would yank her out of the doldrums she'd been stuck in all week. How could she be so angry with Gabriel, yet still miss him so freaking much?

"May I blindfold you?"

"Yes, Sir." She was done with being afraid. Anthony put a black strip of cloth over her eyes and tied it.

"Okay?" he asked.

"Yes." Or maybe not. She couldn't see what he was doing. A shiver went up her spine as she sat and waited.

"This isn't very sharp," he said and ran something metal down her arm.

She tensed up and then relaxed. It wasn't bad. Almost like someone's fingernail running over her skin.

"Now this one is a bit sharper."

Dani inhaled. It was the same feeling. Was Anthony playing with her? Her skin tingled, and her heart pounded, but it wasn't out of fear. While the sensation was the same, it created a shiver of anticipation within her.

"Now, here are several at once." And while he was right—there were several objects on her skin, which weren't rough or hard. Her body heated in wonder. "You're doing great, Dani. One last one."

Dani waited, and the last one touched her skin. A small cry left her lips because it was cold, not because it hurt.

"Crap," Anthony said.

"Sir?" she whispered. There wasn't any pain. Had

something gone wrong?

"It's okay." His breath brushed over her cheek. "I'm going to take the blindfold off, but I want you to know that Gabriel is here, and he doesn't look happy."

As if her heart wasn't already doing a wild beat, it now doubled. Dani nodded, trying to control her emotions. Anthony removed the blindfold, and she blinked several times. "Want to guess what I was using on you?" Anthony asked.

She looked over at his table. "I think at least one of them was the vampire glove." That had to be the one that was several objects.

"Yes, everything else was this." He picked up one of the finger claws, but on this one, the claw was rounded off, so it wasn't sharp.

"You totally played with my mind." Why hadn't she thought of that before now? Because she was feeling the sensations and wishing Gabriel was there. He was, but she hadn't known that.

"That I did. How did you like it?"

"I will say it was different and played with my head a little, but it was a good sensation. Thank you." Not that she'd changed her mind about knife play, but at least she'd gotten an idea of what it might feel like. And she conquered a fear all by herself. She glanced up to see Gabriel next to the stage.

"You are more than welcome." Anthony helped her out of the chair and made sure she was steady on her feet before he released her. "Now, I'll take questions, and if you'd like to come up and see my instruments, you can. All I ask is that you don't handle them."

Dani walked to the stairs. The hard look on Gabriel's face didn't feel encouraging, but she allowed him to help her down the stairs and guide her away.

"Knives are a hard limit," he said, his voice rough.

Well, this wasn't what she thought they needed to talk about, but it was a start. "Yes, but I also put notes by it saying I wanted to watch first and make a decision. That's what I did tonight. Anthony knew exactly what to do."

"So I saw."

"You're angry. Why?"

"Maybe because you allowed another Dom to touch you?"

She straightened. "We haven't talked since last Friday. It was just a demo, and he barely touched me at all except to run his fingers over my skin. Besides, it was Anthony. I have no interest in him."

"Why not? He's good looking."

Dani shook her head. "He is, but he's not my type." Anthony had some rough edges, but so did Gabriel. Everything inside her was calling out to Gabriel, for Gabriel. She put her hand on Gabriel's cheek. "There is only one man I want as my Dom. The problem is, he can't break through his phobia to want me just as much." There! She put it all out there. Ball in his court.

Gabriel huffed with frustration. "I had dinner with my father tonight."

"That was tonight? I'm so sorry." He'd mentioned it a couple of weeks ago but hadn't told her the date. "You should have called me; I would have gone with you." She remembered that dinner with his dad was never fun, even worse with his mother. Was it any wonder Gabriel didn't want to be emotionally or legally committed to one woman? He hadn't had very good role models. Still, Dani had a right to stick up for herself. She wouldn't go on playing this half-in, half-out game. She wanted all of

Gabriel and needed all of him to want her.

"It was better you didn't go." He put his arms around her waist and cradled her close. "I'm sorry I closed you out. I was stunned by what you told me."

"You were angry." All she kept seeing was the anger in his face, his eyes, in his body language.

"Oh, baby." His arms tightened around her. "I wasn't angry at you. I was angry that I couldn't help you through losing the baby."

"I'm sorry I didn't tell you sooner. Things were so crazy at college, and I left for San Francisco."

"I know. It wasn't your fault."

Her body sagged against his. "It took me a long time to accept I wasn't at fault."

"How could you think that? You weren't even aware you were pregnant."

"I know; the doctor told me the same thing. It was just hard."

"Then I spring kink on you without a single explanation." He rested his forehead against hers. "I'm sorry."

Dani accepted his apology into her heart, her body, her soul. She couldn't leave Gabriel. Not when he was working so hard to make up for every misstep in their past. But she had a right to stick up for herself and her love. Yet something inside her softened. She wanted a commitment from him, maybe him being her Dom was the most he could give her. Could she settle for that? Dani imagined a life without Gabriel and knew she'd never be the same if she didn't at least try to make this work for both their sakes. Yes, she would find a way to make it work.

"What about us?" Gabriel whispered.

"What about us?"

"How do we proceed?"

Making her decision, she answered him. "Like we have been." She wasn't going to push him for something he couldn't give her. Not anymore. Maybe one day she would, but for now she wanted Gabriel in her life. She loved him too much to let something he was afraid of get in their way.

Well, damn, she'd really never stopped loving him. He was her man regardless if they were together or not. Dani didn't want anyone else.

"Are you sure?"

"Yes." She wasn't a hundred percent sure of anything, but the last few days without Gabriel had made her realize how much she wanted him in her life. She'd take him as she could get him. Dani glanced at the clock behind the bar. "It's after ten; I need to get home. I've got work tomorrow."

"Let's go."

* * * *

The next two weeks were busy with work. Dani finished up the last Max and Sierra's backyard, and the Wicked Sanctuary job was almost done. Dani smiled as Max signed off on the job. In the past few weeks, her business had exploded, and she'd been busier than ever. Not surprising as a lot of people wanted their yards and plants done during summer.

It made her happy she could keep the family business running. She talked with her grandfather about expanding the business, hiring more people, and maybe getting a bigger office. He told her to do what she wanted, that it was her business now. He was stronger and wanted to enjoy his retirement.

She'd cried when he told her that. Her grandparents had always surrounded her with love and understanding.

And then there was Gabriel.

They'd had dinner with her grandparents last Sunday. It made her heart hurt. She wanted what her grandparents had. A marriage based on love, trust, and happiness. But deep down, she also knew that Gabriel wasn't a man who could commit. Mention marriage, and he'd run for the hills.

She understood. His parents had divorced and remarried so many times. Gabriel had to live with that, and he saw marriage as something one could just throw away. Heck, they'd had already been on marriage three and four when she and Gabriel were in college. Her heart ached for him. For herself.

Dani walked into her apartment just as her cell went off. Gabriel. "Hey," she said.

"Hi, babe, I'm going to run home, shower, and change. Pick you up in an hour?"

"Okay." That would barely give her enough time to do what she needed to do.

* * * *

"Where are we going to dinner?" she asked as he pulled out of the parking spot. She'd managed to be ready when Gabriel arrived.

"Surprise."

Dani grinned at him, especially when they pulled up in front of the Double D BBQ. "How did you know I was in the mood for some good barbecue?"

"When aren't you?" He laughed.

It was true. She loved barbecue. Once they ordered, she looked at Gabriel, really looked. "Are you okay to play tonight?" she asked. He seemed tired.

"I'm fine. It's been a long week. We're almost finished with the expansion of the club. It's been a big job."

"I can't wait for the big unveiling Max keeps talking

about."

"It won't be for a few weeks yet." He leaned over to her. "A birdy told me he's got some new equipment coming in."

Dani flushed. Gabriel loved teasing her about how many ways he could tie her up and make her climax. Then he'd show her. She had to admit Gabriel had been very attentive and loving since the night of Anthony's demo.

They talked about their work week as they ate. "How do you feel about taking our play up a notch tonight?" he asked.

"What do you have in mind?" Their play had been pretty much in line with her limits. Gabriel didn't push even if she wanted him to.

"What do you think about starting off with our standard flogger, moving up to a medium flogger, and if you want more, I'll move to a braided flogger."

She tilted her head. He'd actually said he'd go a little heavier with her? Nice. She'd been wanting this for a while now. Especially with Gabriel. "I'm game."

"All right. That's the plan for tonight."

Dani wiggled in her seat, not sure she could wait.

* * * *

Gabriel watched Dani as she worked with Ralph behind the desk. He stepped into reception after being in the club for a bit. He wanted to be close to Dani. It was Friday night and busy. When hadn't the club been busy lately? It was one of the reasons for the expansion.

It would be nice when they could unveil the new area. There were whispers around the club about what Max had planned. When asked, Gabriel would just smile and tell them to wait and find out. He wasn't going to spoil Max's surprise.

At nine, Dani stood and stretched before she walked over to him. "All done," she said. He admired the deep red corset and black boy shorts she wore and the way she'd piled her hair up.

"Good." He took her hand and led her into the club. The music tonight was more intense heavy metal than normal, but overall, it gave a good beat.

"I reserved the St. Andrew's cross for ten." He was looking forward to playing with Dani.

"Yes, Sir." She gazed around the club, and waved at some of the other subs. With his arm around her waist, Gabriel guided her to the bar where several of the couples sat. His fingers were itching to get down to business.

How would Dani take a braided flogger? It was heavier than they'd used before and would have a heavy impact on her ass. He'd planned carefully and would make sure she was well warmed up before he used it. They sat and talked with several couples when one of the Doms approached him.

"Excuse me, Gabriel."

"Yes, James." Gabriel turned to the man. James was on the smaller size, about five eight, probably weighed around one seventy-five.

"I'm going to go talk with Allyson," Dani said and left the two men alone.

"I'm sorry to bother you, but Colby isn't here tonight, and I was hoping someone could demo the bullwhip for me. I've been wanting to learn how to use one."

Gabriel frowned. "Bullwhips can be dangerous." He rarely worked with whips anymore. He'd kept his skill up with private sessions using a dummy, but not with live subs.

"They can be, but my sub really wants to try." James motioned to a woman standing nearby, shifting from one foot to the other. "Master Max said you'd be the best one to ask."

Gabriel glanced over James' shoulder and saw Max in the back of the club clearing it out. Max was on board. "All right, but I'll need to talk with your sub and Max before I show you. Meet you in the back in five minutes."

"Of course." James walked over to his sub, and they headed over to Max.

Gabriel turned to find Dani only to see she was alone and watching him. He walked over to her. "James asked me to use a bullwhip on his sub. She wants to know what it feels like, and Colby isn't here tonight." He took her hand in his. "The demo won't interfere with our time."

She frowned at him. "I'm not sure I'm comfortable with that. Why can't I be your sub?"

"I just stated his sub wants to feel it." What was she getting at?

"But I'm your sub."

Gabriel opened his mouth and then shut it. "No." He wouldn't use a bullwhip on her; she wasn't ready. "We talked about this, remember. Sometimes Doms will ask me to demo on their subs. Max specifically asked me to do this."

Her eyes grew stormy. "And you said we would discuss it."

"Like you did when you demoed with Anthony?" Why was he bringing that up? He understood why she did what she did. He might not have liked it, but he hadn't been acting like her Dom at the time.

"So when it's convenient for you, I'm your sub, but I'm not allowed to try something with another Dom."

"That's not what I meant." Damn, she took that the wrong way. Not totally her fault he couldn't seem to find the right words.

"You weren't upset when I played with Anthony even if it was a demo and something on my hard limits?"

"I was." He wasn't going to deny it. "We hadn't talked about it as agreed."

"How could I? You weren't at the club, and we weren't exactly talking."

"You know why." Why were they going over this again? Hadn't they moved on?

"I do. I need to know. How committed are you to me, Gabriel?"

He froze. How did he answer that? He enjoyed being with Dani in and out of the club. He was committed to her as he could be. They were in a relationship. Was she talking marriage commitment?

"Your silence is telling." She bit her lower lip. "If you're unwilling to discuss my feelings around this, you've violated our agreement."

He placed his hand on her arm before she could move away. "I can use a dummy for the demo." It would mean the sub wouldn't get to feel the sting of the whip, but if it stopped Dani from walking away until he could figure out why she wasn't listening to him.

The look she gave him was glacial. He shivered. "How is that a demo?"

"I'm not going to use you, Dani." No way in hell. "We haven't gone beyond cow suede; the braided flogger is about as heavy as I'll go with you."

"Why? Because you think I can't handle it?"

"It's not a matter of handling it. Dani, you're a novice with impact play. You have to build up to certain things, not just jump to the top."

"Are you saying you're going to hurt the sub?"

"Whips can take skin. I'm careful, but I'm putting my foot down on this." Why didn't she get that he couldn't use something that heavy on her? What if she moved when he didn't expect it? What if he hurt her? It was one of her hard limits, and he was respecting that. This was one line he wouldn't cross. "I'm sorry, but no to you being my sub for the demo."

"It's over." She shook off his hold and walked toward the doors to the club.

"Like hell." Gabriel slipped off his stool and caught up with her. "Dani, don't do this." He turned her to face him and was dismayed to see tears in her eyes. "Baby?" He cupped her cheek.

"No." She moved away from his touch. "I can't do this."

"Dani." He slipped his arm around her waist. "I love you."

She stiffened in his hold. "Bastard," she whispered. "I won't be manipulated by your words. Red."

Gabriel dropped his arm and watched her turn and march out of the club. Regina was right behind her—after glaring at him. What the hell had just happen? How had he lost control of the situation?

Chapter 9

Dani could barely see through her tears. Damn Gabriel. Why couldn't he understand she needed to be his sub. Maybe she was the fool here? But seeing him work with the whip, knowing what it could do… She shook her head. There had to be someone else in the club that could do the demo?

Her locker finally beeped, and she pulled out her clothes and pulled them over her outfit. How was she going to get home? Max didn't allow them to call for a rideshare to or from the club. It was a safety issue for him.

"Do you need any help?" Dani turned to see Regina standing there.

"I…I…" A sob escaped her lips.

Regina enfolded her in her arms, and Dani cried.

"I need a ride home; I came with Gabriel," she said after several minutes.

"Dane and I can take you home." Regina found a box of tissues and handed several to her.

"Thanks." Dani mopped her eyes and blew her nose. "I knew Gabriel was stubborn but not this bad."

Regina laughed. "All men are. They just need to learn that we women aren't as fragile as they think."

"I'm not fragile. He just thinks I am because of the way I reacted when we were in college." He kept thinking she couldn't let that go but she had. She'd forgiven him. He was the one holding onto that memory. Dani gathered up the rest of her belongings as Regina dressed.

When they walked out of the ladies' room, Dani's heart sank. Dane stood there but no Gabriel. She had hoped… Disappointment hit her low in the gut. He had truly abandoned her this time. Without a word, Dane gestured for them to proceed him.

Regina led her out to an SUV and climbed in back with her. "Don't you want to sit up front with Dane?" Dani asked.

"It's fine. Talk to Regina," Dane said as he started the vehicle.

They talked quietly as Dane drove to Dani's apartment after getting her address. By the time she they arrived at her apartment, she felt better. Still miserable, but better. Her relationship with Gabriel was over. Tonight showed her that. He didn't trust her. Didn't think her opinion counted. And he'd used the "L" word. How low could a man go? Thank goodness she was done with the landscaping at the club and Max's house.

"Thank you for the ride home," Dani said, slipping out of the SUV.

"I should walk you to your door," Dane said with a frown.

"I'm fine. It was kind of you to drive me home." Dani shut the door and walked to her building. She went through the security door and made sure it locked behind her. Dane waited until she was behind that door before he drove off.

Dani made her way to her apartment. Everything in her hurt. Her head, her heart. It was a good thing this was Friday. She turned off her phone before she went to take a shower. She needed to be alone and figure out what she was going to do. Because her heart was shattered. She loved Gabriel, always had, always would.

* * * *

"Dani, honey, would you come in here for a minute," her grandmother asked as she came through the door a week later.

"Of course." Dani set her purse down. She fled her apartment last Saturday after Gabriel wouldn't stop calling or stopping by. "What's up?" she asked, seeing her grandparents seated together on the sofa with worried expressions.

"We're worried about you," her grandmother said as Dani sat in the chair across from them.

"I'm fine. Just a little tired." A lot actually. She'd barely slept since last weekend. She worked fourteen hour days so she could avoid Gabriel as much as possible. He wasn't making it easy. He'd stopped by the business; called her, texted her. Heck, he'd even tried to video chat.

"Dani, you're not happy. If you want out from under the business, it's fine. We can sell it," her grandfather said.

"Absolutely not." Dani stared at her grandparents. "I love the business."

"But you've been so unhappy this week," her grandmother said.

Dani kept quiet. She hadn't told her grandparents about Gabriel and the falling out they had. They hadn't asked why she staying with them this week. "It isn't because of the business." She took a deep breath. "Gabriel and I had a fight."

"Oh?" Her grandfather stiffened.

"I'm sorry to hear that," her grandmother said. "I'm sure things will work out. Did you know that Gabriel checked in on us while you were gone?"

"He did?"

"Yes, and he always asked about you," her grandfather said.

That was news to her. Gabriel never mentioned that he'd asked about her. Only that he'd kept an eye on her grandparents and helped them when they needed it.

"Gabriel loves you," her grandmother said.

"That might be true, but I can't take the chance. He shattered my heart once, and I don't think I could take it a second time." Who was she kidding? Her heart was already in pieces, and she couldn't figure out how to put it back together.

"You're welcome to stay here. Take as much time as you need, but listen to your heart, Dani," her grandmother said.

"Thanks, both of you." Dani stood and made her way out into the garden. This was where she'd first fallen in love with horticulture, watching her grandfather tend these flowers and bushes. Being here calmed her.

* * * *

Later that Friday evening, Dani walked into Wicked Sanctuary. She might look like death warmed over, but she told Max she'd be there to help Ralph. She'd begged off last Saturday night, but she wouldn't do that to Max a second time.

Ralph gave her a sharp look, but Dani just smiled and did her job, and when things were manageable for Ralph, she left.

Saturday night rolled around, and she walked into the club feeling a little better. Being here calmed the turmoil she was feeling. As the members came in, she could tell there was a different feel in the air, and she wondered what was going on.

It was also busier than usual. She didn't get done until almost nine-thirty when Allyson came to get her. Ralph told her to go have fun.

"I know we've talked, but are you okay?" Allyson asked as she pulled Dani toward the sub area.

"I'm better." She'd told Allyson more today about what happened with her and Gabriel. It had helped her process the rest of her feelings.

"Good."

"Ah, there's our missing sub," Lara said.

"Not missing, just took a little bit of break," Dani said, sitting down. She missed this, being with other women who understood.

"I'm glad you're back," Regina said.

"Thanks for covering for me last Saturday." Regina had been the one to call her Saturday morning and suggest Dani take a break, and she'd cover the front desk with Ralph.

After chatting for a while, Colby joined them. "Dani, I've been asked to do a demo with an implement that Lara isn't comfortable with. Can I borrow you again?"

"Which implement?" she asked.

"Bison flogger."

Dani didn't even hesitate. "Sure." A good flogging would help her clear her head even more. She was tired of thinking about what to do about Gabriel. There was no solution. She had to let him go.

"Wonderful." Colby held his hand out to her.

* * * *

Gabriel strode into the club at ten, knowing Dani wouldn't be behind the desk. He slipped into the club and over to the bar. There she was, sitting and chatting with the other subs. Good. He'd tried all week to talk to her, but she'd refused.

She wouldn't answer his calls, his texts, or anything he tried. He'd even sent her flowers. She hadn't stayed after her shift last night. He kept his gaze on her. She looked tired. Probably no more than he was.

When Colby held his hand out to her, Gabriel stiffened. His gaze followed them. When Colby helped Dani onto a stage that held a bondage horse, he stood up.

"No." Max stepped in front of him.

"Max…" Gabriel started.

"She called her safe word last week, and you acted like an ass," Max said.

"He's been told that," Zeke commented. "Multiple times, by me."

Gabriel glared at Zeke, but deep down, he knew Zeke was right. He had reacted badly to Dani's request. Why hadn't he just told James he couldn't do the demo? When Dani walked out on him last week, something broke inside him. While he tried to reach her all week, he'd also spent the week taking a long, hard look at what he'd said and what had happened.

"Fine. I was an ass." Gabriel tried to shake off Max's hold.

"I'm not letting you go. I want you to stand here and watch. I mean *really* watch."

"Come on, Max." He couldn't watch Dani play with another Dom. That would be torture.

"No, Gabriel, if you wish to remain in my club, you will stand here and watch the demo."

"Hard ass," Gabriel muttered. If it was the only way he could stay, he'd do it.

"And don't you forget it."

Gabriel nodded, rested his ass against the bar stool, and kept his gaze on the stage. Colby was chatting with Dani, but she hadn't removed any of her clothing. Good. Not that she was wearing much, just a sports bra and a pair of boy shorts.

Colby had Dani lean over the bondage horse, but he didn't restrain her. He picked up a rabbit flogger, explaining to the crowd this was to warm up the sub. And how a sub would usually either be naked or at least half undressed, but since this wasn't his sub, he was respecting her wishes.

Interesting. Before, when Colby flogged her, Dani had removed her top. What was different tonight? After a few passes with the first flogger, he picked up the next one, suede and leather.

"Look at her face," Max whispered.

Gabriel's gaze shifted. What the hell? Dani's eyes were wide open. With him, she would already be primed and emotional. There was no expression on her face at all. This was not the Dani he was used to seeing. Something wasn't right.

Colby switched to a bison flogger. It had wider falls so would be thuddy and not stinging. As he flogged Dani's butt, she had no reaction at all. A wince here and there, but nothing big. Oh yes, something was off for sure. His woman was not enjoying this.

"I can't continue to let this happen," he muttered, and he strode toward the stage. No one stopped him this time.

Colby shifted his attention as Gabriel mounted the stage and nodded. "It's about time," he muttered.

Gabriel ignored him and walked over to Dani. "Sweetheart," he said, laying his hand on her cheek. "Baby, you are not enjoying this, are you?"

"Not really, Sir."

With the 'sir' his breath caught. "But you've enjoyed this with me."

Dani closed her eyes but not before he saw the misery

in them. "So?" Her tone was flat yet defiant.

"Do you want me to flog you?"

Her eyes widened. After a long minute, when his heart almost stopped, she answered him, "Yes, Sir. Please."

His heart lightened. She reacted to him. He ran his hand over her back to her boy shorts. "These need to come off."

"Yes, Sir."

The way she was positioned over the spanking horse, it was easy for him to remove her shorts, and to add a little extra, he restrained her legs.

Gabriel rubbed her ass before he stepped back. Colby gestured to the table. Gabriel's bag sat there. "I think I've been set up," he muttered.

Colby just grinned. "I'll do a running commentary from the floor." He hopped off the stage. "Gabriel is going to take over with his sub."

Gabriel took a deep breath to center himself as he pulled his floggers out. Bison, cow suede, and braided. Packed the week before and never touched since. He picked up the bison flogger. Dani was relaxed over the spanking horse. Good.

"He's starting off with the bison flogger. The only reason he can start with that is because his sub is already warmed up."

Gabriel let the flogger fly, and Dani released a small moan. Two more strikes, and he stopped, rubbing her ass. He could hear Colby talking, but his focus was all on Dani. "I'm going to use the cow suede next," he whispered to her.

"Yes, Sir." Her voice was soft, but there was no distress.

Ten swats with the cow suede flogger and she'd gone up and down on her toes for each of them. He rubbed her ass—a nice, red color now—every two to three hits. "How are you doing?"

Her eyes were closed, her breathing rapid. "Fine, Sir."

"Open your eyes, sweetheart." She did. They were clear and filled with desire. "I really do love you, Dani." He leaned over and kissed her.

"I love you too." Her voice was soft.

A sense of contentment enveloped Gabriel. One he hadn't felt since he was with Dani in college. Gabriel stepped back, letting all the worry and fear go. He trusted Dani as much as she trusted him. She was his, and it was past time he gave her what she wanted.

* * * *

Dani closed her eyes when Gabriel stepped away. Her body was so hot and needy. So different from when Colby flogged her. She'd been going through the motions with Colby, but with Gabriel…she couldn't.

They might have had a week apart, but her body craved his touch. The flogger hit her ass, and she gasped. He was using the braided flogger. She was sure of it.

The other two floggers were warmups for this one. At the second swat, her nerves jumped and tingled. While there was a moment of pain, it disappeared quickly. Gabriel rubbed her ass, then another hit came.

By the time he hit ten, she was moaning constantly. Her body was floating and her muscles lax. This was what she needed…from the right person. Two more swats, and he rubbed her ass again. She was starting to drift into that blissful state.

"So beautiful." His body pressed against hers. The pressure made her blood sing. His lips caressed her back. "I'm going to undo your wrists."

"Yes, Sir." Part of her was disappointed he wasn't

continuing with the flogging, but another part knew it was time to stop. She wasn't in subspace yet but darn close. Gabriel moved, and a blanket was placed over her back.

He kept a hand on the small of her back as he undid the ankle restraints, and she was in his arms. She snuggled into his hold, so happy to be back in his embrace. As he walked off the stage, she could hear people talking to him, but the words didn't make sense.

In the aftercare area, he sat and carefully cradled her in his lap. "You were fantastic." He dropped kisses over her face.

"I…" She shifted and winced as a flash of awareness shot through her body. Oh, she was going to be sore for a few days.

"Lara, would you get the blue tube from my bag and bring it to me, please?"

"Of course, Sir."

"What is Lara getting?" Her brain was starting to come out of the haze.

"Something that will help you not be so sore tomorrow." He gazed down at her. "Coming out of subspace?"

"Yes. I wasn't fully there. My body feels like it's on fire." Heat filled every nook of her. A good heat.

"I'm not surprised." Lara returned, and Gabriel took the tube from her with a thank you. "Okay, up and over my lap."

Dani groaned. She'd rather stay cradled in his arms, but she did as he asked. Her legs were steadier than she expected. She laid over his lap, feeling a little emotionally exposed.

"This cream will help with the soreness." She yelped as the cold hit her hot skin. "Sorry." There was laughter in his voice. Slowly, he rubbed the cream in. Two more times, he added more. By the time he was done, her ass didn't feel as bad.

"Now, we're going to talk."

"Like this?" She was still over his lap.

"Yes, so if I don't like your answers, I can do this." He swatted her where her thighs and ass met.

"Sir!" Damn. It didn't hurt, but it made her nerves start dancing and craving more.

"I'm going to tell you something, and I want you to listen to me."

"Of course, Sir."

"I couldn't—no, make that wouldn't—use the bullwhip on you. It's a hard limit for you, and James' request wasn't like Anthony's demo. Anthony took your fear into consideration, and that's what I was doing. I knew a whip wouldn't be good for you."

"Why didn't you tell me this?"

"I tried, but apparently, I didn't explain myself well enough. I need to work on my communication with you." He shook his head. "I can also be an ass who doesn't think." When she raised her head, he swatted her ass. "I will have one the subs who likes the bullwhip talk to you about it, but that's as far as it goes."

"Yes, Sir." She was still a touch wary, but she would accept some responsibility. "I'm sorry I pushed and didn't fully listen."

"This is my cross to bear, not yours." He continued to rub her back. "I also let my own insecurities get to me." In a flash, she was flipped upright in his lap.

"How did you do that, Sir?" Her head spun.

"Secret trick." He cradled her close. "I'm sorry I didn't talk with you before agreeing and for not explaining properly. Lord knows I'm going to make mistakes in this relationship, but know that I meant what I said. I do love you, Dani."

"I know." She believed him. Gabriel wouldn't lie to her about that. It had taken her time to work it all through her head and heart.

"Good. I've spent a lot of time this last week thinking about everything."

"Oh?" She sat up.

"Relax, baby. I reacted badly when you told me about the baby. You didn't even know you were pregnant when you lost her."

"Her?"

"Yes, I pictured a little girl with her mother's sass." He took a deep breath. "I forced myself to look at my life and my choices. Dani, you were and will always be my best choice. I'm not like my parents."

"Of course you aren't." Was he finally coming to the realization? She'd known it for years.

"When you pulled away in college, I let you because I truly believed I couldn't commit to one woman, but now—" He ran his fingers over her face.

"Now?"

"I love you, and while it scares me, I am committed to you and only you. I probably have been since college. I was just too stubborn to see it."

"Oh, Gabriel." She looped her arms around his neck.

"I felt you pulling away and thought maybe you needed something more."

"I was lost in my own head. It wasn't until after I left for San Francisco that I talked with someone. I should have told you."

He put his fingers over her lips. "It's okay."

She nodded. "I don't want to push you into a commitment. Knowing you love me is more than enough." It was. He hadn't said the words back then, but he had tonight, and she was going to put her trust in him and his words.

"I'm glad you did. It made me think." He gazed down at her. "Can we start over one more time? This time, I promise not to be an ass but the man you love."

"Gabriel, I've never stopped loving you. I've always loved you."

"Yes," he shouted, and did a fist pump before he lowered his head to capture her lips with his. When they both came up for air, they were surrounded by their friends.

"It's about time," Allyson said.

Dani's face grew hot, along with her body. She gathered the blanket around her lower half. Gabriel chuckled, but helped her.

"Who says you can't teach an old Dom new tricks?" Sierra quipped.

"Who are you calling old?" Max glared at her.

"No one, Sir." Her eyes twinkled with mischief.

"You two have ten minutes before I unveil the expansion," Max said, and took Sierra's arm and led her away.

"Oh boy, Sierra is going to have a sore ass tonight," Crystal's observation was met with unanimous agreement.

"I need to find my shorts and put them on," Dani whispered.

"Here you go." Tessa dropped them into her lap.

Dani closed her eyes and groaned.

"No embarrassment. We're all family here," Lara said.

Family. That felt right. Dani looked at Gabriel. He looked a little stunned. Their friends dispersed, so Dani stood with the blanket around her and slipped on her shorts. Her ass protested the fabric, but she liked the little tingles flowing through her body. It reminded her of how much Gabriel cared for her. Enough to give her what she needed.

It also reminded her of who she belonged to. Gabriel. Yes, she belonged to him. "Let me put the blanket in the used basket." She made her way to the basket and back to Gabriel in record time. Hand in hand, they walked over to where everyone stood.

Max stood at the midpoint of a big plastic sheet, with Jordan at one end and Damon at the other. "As you know, we"—he nodded to Jordan and Damon—"decided to expand the club. Zeke and Gabriel did a fantastic job with the plans and construction. Dani did all the landscaping. Let's thank them."

The crowd clapped and called out words of thanks and great work. Max held his hands up. "Tonight, I'm going to unveil the new part of our club. In the next few weeks, on Thursday nights, demos will be given on the new equipment. No one can use the equipment until they've attended the demos."

Max gripped the plastic, along with Jordan and Damon, they pulled. The plastic fell.

Dani couldn't help but gasp. The new area was filled with equipment she hadn't seen before. There was a row of rooms with numbers on the doors and a new back door with a sign that said, "Play Garden."

"As you can see, we have some new and exciting equipment, but also four rooms that can be enjoyed for some privacy."

"What is the Play Garden?" someone asked.

"That is a special place where we're going to have some parties and other fun. Let's just say, the Doms will have fun; the subs might not."

Groans and chuckles reached her ears, and Dani grinned. Leave it to Max to tantalize everyone.

Gabriel turned and tugged her away from the crowd. "I think I'm going to like the Play Garden," he said, pulling her into his arms.

"I bet." She rested against him, loving the feel of his body against hers.

"Dani, I want to be with you every part of every day. I want to share the best of each day and help you through the worst. Will you move in with me?"

Her eyes widened, and she tilted her head up. She could see the fear in his eyes and loved him even more for pushing through it. "Yes, I will."

He grinned and lowered his mouth to hers.

Dani leaned into his kiss. This is where she wanted to be. In Gabriel's arms, his life, and with him always.

Thank you for reading *Tantalize,* the sixth book in the Wicked Sanctuary series. If you enjoyed this book, please consider leaving a review on Goodreads, or your retailer, and know that it would be greatly appreciated.

For new release information and news about Marie Tuhart, please join her newsletter.

If you enjoyed *Tantalize, Edged* will be released in spring of 2023.

ABOUT THE AUTHOR

Marie Tuhart lives in the beautiful Pacific Northwest. She loves to read and write, and when she's not writing, she spends time with her two dogs, Tommy and Trina, family, traveling and enjoying life.

Marie is a multi-published author with The Wild Rose Press and Trifecta Publishing, and is self-published. To be alerted to her new releases, you can join Marie's newsletter or check out her website: www.mairetuhart.com

OTHER BOOKS BY MARIE TUHART

Her Desert Prince (Desert Destiny)

Her Desert Doctor (Desert Destiny)

Her Desert Horseman (Desert Destiny)

Her Desert Protector (Desert Destiny)

Highland Dom (McMillan Passion)

Bound & Teased

Claimed by the Sheikh

Billionaire's Cowboy's Conquest

More of You (Club Crave)

Reflections of you (Club Crave)

Bound to Love You (Club Crave)

Hot for You (Club Crave)

Tempt (Wicked Sanctuary Series)

Entice (Wicked Sanctuary Series)

Seduce (Wicked Sanctuary Series)

Ravish (Wicked Sanctuary Series)

Possess (Wicked Sanctuary Series)

Tantalize (Wicked Sanctuary Series)

Zodiac Encounters - Astrology Anthology: Aries and Leo

Edged (Wicked Sanctuary Series) Spring 2023

PREVIEW OF *EDGED*

Kaley Clark parked her Fluff and Puff van outside the house, surprised when her client, Clara Pierce, wasn't outside waiting for her. That was unusual. Kaley got out and smiled, proud of the decal wrap on her van. Dogs, cats, and contact information in a park setting covered the sides, back, and top. It had cost her a pretty penny, but she loved it.

Tapping the springer spaniel leaping through the air in the picture, Kaley secured her shoulder length auburn hair and made her way to the front door, hoping Clara was all right. Nugget, Clara's Maltipoo, barked, reassuring Kaley.

The door opened and…Kaley took a step back.

Anthony, or Payne as they called him in the club, stood there, his black hair mussed, and his blue eyes dazed. Her heart sped up. Sexy didn't begin to describe this man. "Can I help you?" His deep voice sent shivers up her spine.

"I'm—"

"It's Kaley. Let her in, Anthony. Remember? She's here to groom Nugget."

"You're the dog groomer?"

Kaley bit the inside of her lower lip so she didn't smile. "I don't know why everyone seems surprised to find out I'm the dog groomer."

"Maybe because you'd make the perfect model for painting," he said, holding the door open so she could enter.

"I don't think so." She laughed off his comment. Kaley was aware she was average looking, nothing special.

"I'm in the family room, dear. Don't let my grandson distract you," Clara's voice rang out strong and clear.

"Is she okay?" Kaley asked in a low voice.

"Sprained ankle. She's been told to stay off of it." He shut the door as Kaley walked down the small hallway. Nugget started whining and wiggling when she saw Kaley. "Hi Clara," she said, seeing the woman sitting with her leg propped up on a pillow, trying to hold on to the energetic dog.

"Allow me," Anthony said, maneuvering around her to remove the baby gate across the doorway. "We're trying to keep Nugget confined to this room."

"I see." Kaley slipped by him and swore she smelled paint and turpentine. If she remembered right, Anthony was an artist. He also did demos at Wicked Sanctuary. Kaley's heart pounded with thoughts about all the times she'd watched his intense sessions, never sure she was up for his brand of play. Deep down, some feral part of her wanted to step up and try, though she'd never had the courage.

Nugget jumped out of Clara's arms and launched herself at Kaley. "Easy, Nugget." Kaley caught the dog as she jumped into her arms. Laughter bubbled up as she was given doggy kisses all over her face.

"Nugget," Clara admonished.

"It's fine," Kaley said, tightening her arms around Nugget so the small dog didn't fall. "Are you in pain, Clara? I could have done this on another day."

"It's nothing." Clara waved her hands. "Doctor's being cautious."

"Doctor is making sure you heal," Anthony said, giving Clara a pointed look.

Kaley's knees weakened. There it was, that Dom stare. Oh yes, she'd seen him around Wicked Sanctuary, and she'd kept her distance. He seemed a little too intense for her, but that didn't stop her lady bits from taking notice.

"The usual?" she asked Clara. She was here to groom the dog, not make eyes at Anthony, no matter what her body said.

"Oh yes, dear. That would be wonderful."

"All right. I'll ring the bell when I'm done." Kaley turned.

"I'll walk you out," Anthony said, putting his hand on her elbow.

Tingles flowed from her elbow throughout her body. This wasn't fair. She didn't want to react to him this way but couldn't seem to control herself.

He opened the door for her. "Do you need anything?" he asked.

"Just Nugget."

"Shame," he whispered. "Maybe when you're done with Nugget I can have a moment of your time?"

She frowned. "Why?"

His grin caused her heart hit high gear again.

"To talk."

"Talk?" Now she sounded like a parrot. "I'm not sure we have anything to talk about."

"I think we might."

Kaley shook her head and walked to her van. Nope. Not going to happen. He already tilted her equilibrium, and she wasn't model material no matter what he thought.

* * * *

Anthony Pierce watched the pretty dog groomer hurry to her van. Fluff and Puff. He grinned as he closed the door. Kaley seemed familiar to him, while her business name wasn't. He could have seen her or met her around town.

Maybe at his gallery opening. The opening had been

filled with people. Not his favorite thing. He disliked cloying crowds, but he had to keep up appearances, so he'd done the opening. A grin slid over his lips. Kaley may have laughed off his comment about her being his model, but he wasn't kidding. He wanted to paint her.

"How long will the grooming take?" he asked his grandmother.

"About an hour." Clara picked up her book.

"Okay, I'm going to go back and paint for a bit." The image of Kaley was implanted in his head, and he was itching to put her into his latest work.

"Go."

Making his way to the sunroom, which had become his temporary workspace, Anthony glanced at his work. When his grandmother sprained her ankle, the doctor said she needed to stay off of it until it healed, which could be up to two weeks.

Anthony had immediately moved into the main house with her. There was a cottage on his grandmother's property he'd lived in since he was eighteen, when his parents threw him out. He shook his head, unwilling to give much thought to that time in his life. He'd been confused and set adrift. Luckily, his grandmother took him in and gave him the time to come into himself.

Stepping inside the sunroom, he put a new canvas on the stand and began sketching. His muse took over, and his fingers tingled at being back at work again. Between the gallery opening and the club, he hadn't had much time to paint. He picked up some charcoal and began sketching the chaise lounge in his mind. Anthony's body heated as an image of a woman started to form.

An unusual reaction when he was sketching. It was Kaley. Something about her pulled at him. Once she was finished with Nugget, they would talk. He wanted her as his model, and it was the first time in a very long time he wanted to spend time with a woman.